WICKED GAMES

USA TODAY bestselling author

RENEE HARLESS

WICKED GAMES

USA TODAY bestselling author

RENEE HARLESS

I played the game.
There were rules.
There was strategy.
There was always an escape.

No one knew how my past dictated my every move.
I did everything to keep the nightmares of my childhood
at bay.
I reveled in my playboy reputation.

Then Sarah Hodges made a wrong move.
One that left me wondering how to match her play.

We weren't supposed to work.
She was everything I wasn't.
But she had secrets of her own.
Ones that left me shocked and furious.
Ones that gave me a leg up.
Or so I thought.

It only took one quick game to land us in checkmate,
something Wellington University never saw coming.

CHAPTER ONE

SARAH

I feared this day would arrive, had been counting on it since the spring, but nothing could have prepared me to find the large envelope with the legal header in the corner.

I didn't even need to open it to know what waited for me inside on heavy cardstock. The contents were life-changing and not in a good way.

My hand shook as I closed the small metal door to my mailbox and stowed the letter and junk mail into my backpack as I made the trek back to my dorm. My feet shuffled along on auto pilot, and with each step, the weight on my chest grew heavier to the point where I felt like I was suffocating by the time I reached the middle of the campus.

I had no idea what I was going to do and the only shred of hope that I had remaining was that the letter would offer some sort of guidance. But even I knew that it was unlikely.

The summer air in the small town outside of Boston, Massachusetts, was thick and intense, matching the turmoil I found myself in. This was the first summer that I was spending on campus, I had until July to move my things from the dorm into a small studio apartment I had found in the same complex as my friend Jolee. I had been living with my friend Keeley in the dorms, both of us being new sophomores to the university this past year. But she had joined a sorority and lived in their housing while it left me struggling to find a place to live that my savings from my previous jobs would help cover.

I needed to start looking for a part-time job over the summer to help cushion my savings even more. My father didn't have enough to help, barely able to make ends meet on his own with the disability checks he received. And we had been fighting against the hospital bills that continued to arrive since my mother's death almost a decade ago.

"Damn," I said as a swift breeze tossed my red hair into my face, the strands sticking to my lip gloss-covered mouth. My wild mane covered my eyes and I missed the step that dropped the sidewalk down toward the fountain at the center of campus.

The burn of the concrete against my palms and knees caused tears to well up on my lower lids. I was grateful that I was able to catch myself; otherwise, I'd most likely have scrapes all over my body that would match my hair color.

At first, I thought that no one witnessed my misstep. Most people tended to ignore me around campus as it is. But just as I pushed myself up to a kneeling position, the cackles started. They started low, like one or two people noticing my trip, then they grew to a large symphony of harmonic giggles.

Of course, the campus couldn't be empty today of all days. It wasn't as if I didn't have enough on my mind. Fate had to add in a hefty dose of embarrassment as well. Not that this was different than any other day. I was a klutz through and through, spending the majority of my time with my head down, making sure that I wasn't tripping or running into anything. Not that it had helped in the past. There was a reason why I only lasted one day as a waitress at the local diner in my hometown. Carrying trays and being clumsy did not go well together. Spilling eight glasses of water on a group of football players and their girlfriends didn't end well for my last few weeks of highschool.

My father told me to walk with my head held high and everyone would ignore my mistakes. That was easier said than done for sure, especially for someone that had social anxiety. Keeping my head down kept my nerves at bay.

I was a mess, literally.

The laughter continued around me and I looked up to find a gaggle of half-dressed girls huddled around a man that leaned against one of the building's railings. The women sneered in my direction as they snickered, the man I recognized as one of the campus' Ridge Rogues didn't laugh, but a smirk tilted the corner of his mouth upward.

If I had a backbone at all, I would tell them where they could all go, but instead, I brushed off my knees as I stood, taking note of the blood dripping from some of the scratches. I was definitely going to feel this in the morning.

Trying not to let the group know how they affected me, I gathered my backpack and pushed my hair away from my face and behind my ears. I stole one last glance at the group, my eyes catching on the gorgeous man in the center. The girls seemed to orbit around him as if he were their sun. With his dirty blond hair and sharp gaze, I could see how they were pulled toward him. He must have noticed me staring because the smirk dropped from his mouth and he cocked an impatient brow in my direction.

I gripped the strap of my backpack tighter in my grasp and turned away, ashamed to have been caught staring at the gorgeous man. My sandal-clad feet twisted up beneath me as I tried to rush away from the scene, almost losing my footing again, but thankful I was able to right myself before another catastrophe occurred.

Hurriedly I rushed toward my dorm at the opposite end of campus, murmuring to myself that I needed to keep my gaze forward and not to turn around to see if the group was still laughing at my retreating back. I didn't need to look; I could feel the guy's gaze penetrating my back with each step that I took.

Finally, I arrived at my dorm, but as I inserted my key in the lock, I struggled to open the door. Keeley never seemed to have this problem, but I did almost everytime. We had even exchanged keys at one point, but the problem didn't seem to be the key, but me.

The room was barren on the side where Keeley had slept. A loft bed pressed against the wall and a single dresser were tucked underneath. My side seemed just as barren, but not for the same reason. I just couldn't afford all of the niceties that every other girl at Wellington University seemed to decorate with. Bed linens, towels, and some clothes were all that I needed to get by.

I knew that I needed to start packing up my things, but it wasn't going to take me long, only two suitcases worth of items. I planned to hit up a local thrift shop for furniture for the apartment, even though Jolee had offered for me to use her things since she spent most of her time with her boyfriend, Ford. Her things were nice, very nice. Jolee's roommate and cousin Willow had purchased the bedroom set with funds from her parents. The furniture was nicer than anything I had ever seen or had for that matter.

Slipping my bag from my shoulders, I tossed it onto my desk and promptly ignored the contents while I heated up a small bowl of mac and cheese in the tiny microwave we were allowed to have on campus. I knew I couldn't overlook the envelope addressed to me much longer, but I knew the outcome was going to remain the same whether I opened it now or five hours later.

I was tempted to call my father to get his advice, but I refrained. I knew exactly what he'd say. He'd work his magic and convince me to come home, that I didn't need to work myself to the grind to pay for the private university that didn't offer anything different than the community college I had transferred from. Accounting classes could be taken anywhere. The appeal of Wellington University wasn't something that my father understood. For me, it was the college my mother had attended and it made me feel closer to her. And the thought of having to leave left a sour taste in my mouth.

My father didn't understand why I needed to travel so far away to feel closer to my mother, but he did his best to act supportive. But I knew deep inside he was lonely and most likely missed having the help at home.

I wasn't ashamed of where and how I grew up. The double-wide trailer my father owned was in a better part of the small mining town. We could walk wherever we needed to go, which I enjoyed but had become increasingly more difficult for my father, who sustained a knee and hip injury while working the mines. But he had friends that offered to take him where he wanted to go. I suspect he was more lonely than anything. I had never left home until I transferred to the college last year.

Turning on the small television I picked up outside of a dumpster once Keeley had left, I found a mindless movie playing and lost myself in the drivel until the anticipation became too much. The envelope was beckoning me to open it and I knew I was only putting off the inevitable.

Dear Ms. Hodges,

We regret to inform you that your Hastings Scholarship has been revoked due to recent unforeseen circumstances. Unfortunately, we will be unable to offer another scholarship in its place. You may begin the process of applying for new financial assistance beginning on June 15th. We apologize for the notice and hope that this news does not deter you from continuing your education with Wellington University. We pride ourselves on the wide range and diversity of our students.

Your current unpaid balance: $56,860 for tuition and fees for the upcoming academic year.

If you are unable to pay the balance by August 3rd, please reach out to your academic dean in written form to withdraw from the university.

I had to read the note four times before the words began to sink in. They offered no other assistance though I had been on the university's Dean's list for the two semesters I attended and was a member of the National

Honor Society and salutatorian at my high school. So much for all of that hard work the last couple of years.

The revoking of the scholarship didn't surprise me. I had heard the rumblings of it happening and the reasoning why. The scholarship, named after Senator Hastings, who donated the funds to three out-of-state students every semester, had come under fire when the Senator died of a heart attack last winter.

Not only did his widow have zero access to the funds to supply the scholarship, but various news sources were also citing claims that the esteemed politician had a nefarious side filled with affairs, extortion, and harassment. Rumor around campus was that Ford, Jolee's boyfriend and one of the Ridge Rogues, was the son of Senator Hastings. I didn't notice the resemblance except in the eyes. Hastings and Ford had the same color eyes – bright blue. But he never confirmed or denied the allegations, which left me wondering if there was indeed any truth to the claims since there was nothing left of the scholarship fund.

With a deep sigh, I tossed the paper onto my bed and fell back onto the overly firm mattress, my body practically bouncing on the tough material. I had very few options at my disposal. Of course, I could easily leave the university, sacrificing my education and my chance at living somewhere new. That seemed like the most likely of options, but there had to be something out there.

Despite not wanting to call my father, I reached for my secondhand cell phone from my back pocket and dialed the number that I knew by heart. The landline number not changing since we moved into the trailer. My father refused to own a cell phone, stuck in his ancient ways.

The phone rang on the other line and I bit my lip, wondering if my father would answer. I knew that he should be home on a Tuesday around 3 p.m., his favorite game show would be on television at that time.

I waited out the rings a few more seconds and pulled the phone from my ear prepared to end the call before the tired voice of my father called out.

"Sarah?"

"Hey, Dad."

"Well, this is an unexpected surprise. To what do I owe this pleasure?"

"Can't a daughter just call her father?" I said in jest.

"Of course, but usually we wait until our weekly call on Sunday."

"True."

"So. . .why the call now? What's going on, dumpling?"

"I have a problem."

My father inhaled sharply before asking, "Are you pregnant?"

"No!" I shouted in explanation. "I don't even have a boyfriend."

"Don't need a boyfriend to get pregnant. Didn't they teach you that in health class?"

He wasn't wrong. I hadn't slept with anyone since I moved to Boston, and before that, it had only been twice with my high school boyfriend. But my father didn't need to know that.

"No, I'm not pregnant, father. I can't believe that you'd suggest it."

"I know. You're my good girl. So, what is it? You can barely tolerate taking over-the-counter pain medication, so I know that it's not drugs. Are you in trouble?"

Not the kind of trouble he suspected.

"No, I'm fine. It has nothing to do with me, physically." I went on to explain the letter I received from financial assistance and the remaining balance for my tuition.

"Oh, Sarah, I'm sorry to hear this. I wish that there was something I could do, someway I could help. I suppose that I could look for some work and help to fit the bill, but I don't think I'd make anywhere close to the dollar amount you'd need in that time frame."

"I know and I'd never ask you for your help. I'm the one that wanted to come here for the program."

"Maybe. . ." Here it was, his plea for me to come home. I was surprised we had made it this far in the conversation before he thought about mentioning it. "Maybe you should come home. You can probably get a job at the bank or babysit again while you take classes at the community college. You know I'd be happy to have you home."

"I know, Dad. It's good to know that I have some place to go. I know not everyone is that lucky. I think I'll put in a few job applications."

"What could you possibly find that will pay you anywhere close to the amount that you need?" he asked, his tone full of frustration.

"I don't know, but I won't ever know if I don't try."

I didn't dare mention that I had an idea of what would pay what I needed, but it was my last resort option and one that I hoped I wouldn't need to entertain.

"Sarah. . ."

"Everything will be fine, Dad. I just wanted to give you a heads up and let you know what was going on."

"Well, you know that I will always welcome you back home, but I'm proud of you for sticking with it, the college thing, I mean. I know growing up here wasn't always the easiest."

It was hard growing up in a small town when everyone knew your business. The place and people could be suffocating with their nosiness and inability to separate a child version of yourself and an adult. The worst was when people knew something long before you did. Half of the town knew that my mom had passed away before I had. And when my father was injured? I found out on the school bus ride home from another student. Those were the things that I hated and why I had wanted to rid myself of the town without a backward glance. Unfortunately, unless I could find a job that paid more than most of the people in my town made in a year, I would be returning home sooner rather than later.

"I love you, Dad. I'll call you on Sunday as scheduled."

"You do that. Good luck, Sarah. And I mean that."

I knew that he meant it despite his desire to want me to come home. My father was always the most supportive person in my life, even if he didn't approve of my taken path.

Grabbing my laptop, I pulled up a university job posting site to see if there were any positions on campus that I could fulfill. It didn't take long to realize that there were no jobs available that could work with my busy class schedule. I needed something that would allow me to work early in the day and late in the evening. My classes filled my daytime schedule and that barely left any time for homework.

My fingers tapped away on the keyboard, bringing up various jobsites, but nothing available in the area I needed to search. I didn't have access to a car and public transport was an expense that I didn't want to waste my money on. Finding a job within walking distance was going to be imperative, except it was also doubtful. Jobs around the university were already claimed or taken by locals. And with my lack of coordination, I knew that waiting tables or serving coffee wasn't options that I had.

Slowly I scrolled through the listings, scoffing at the offerings available. It seemed like I was going to have to huff it on foot to see if any place close by was taking on new employees. At least I knew that I could learn a new task quickly.

Just as I was about to close the screen to my computer a small ad at the bottom of the listings caught my eye. It wasn't an ideal situation, but considering the current circumstances, I knew that I couldn't be overly picky.

Clicking on the ad, I read through the description, trying not to cringe at the details. I needed to remember that my choices were limited and I needed a lot of money and fast. Outside of prostitution, this seemed like my best option. My father would have a field day with the knowledge of what I was about to do. Writing down the address, I plugged it into my phone's GPS and noticed that the location was nowhere within walking distance. I would have to use public transportation, but if I made the promised funds, I wouldn't have to worry about the expense. There was even a chance that I could buy a cheap car to get around.

Glancing down at my outfit, a loose-fitted T-shirt and frayed denim shorts, I rushed to my closet and grabbed the single sundress that I owned, hoping that I'd at least make a good impression visually. Or as good of one as I could. As long as I didn't trip or stumble, I should be okay.

The bus ride into the next town didn't take long, but it dropped me off in an area I was unfamiliar with. I was thankful that the sun was still hanging high in the sky and that I'd had the forethought to have the directions available on my phone.

Walking for two blocks, I found myself in front of a non-descript building. At first, I thought I was in the wrong place, but then a small woman pulled up in an expensive car and parked in front of where I stood.

"Hi, can I help you?"

"Yes, I saw an ad online. I was looking for Alice Sullivan."

"Well, you've found her. Let's go inside and chat."

I dutifully followed the woman into the building and I gasped in shock when the doors closed behind me. The walls were covered in deep purple and black fabrics, giving the open space a luxurious feeling with the brass accents on the table and lights. A bar lined the far side of the room, facing a stage with multi-levels.

The glamorous woman spun around as she placed her designer handbag on a table in the middle of the room. "You're pretty enough, with some work, of course. Now, there is one thing I need you to do so we can get it out of the way."

My hands shook. I knew what was coming and my nerves were at an all-time high. Nervously I wiped my sweaty palms against the fabric at my thighs.

"Yes, ma'am. What is it you need me to do?"

With a gentle nod and smile, Alice angled her head toward the stage. "Dance."

RENEE HARLESS

CHAPTER TWO

SARAH

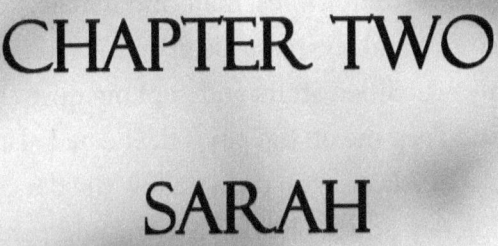

My body ached as I set out for an early morning run. When Alice hired me, she immediately put me on a new exercise routine. She said that I needed to increase my energy and stamina. She also sent one of the other employees to my apartment to teach me how to apply the makeup I would wear on stage. The other dancer, Stephanie, was a student at another university working her way to a law degree. We had talked and found that she and I had found ourselves in similar predicaments and needed money fast. Of course, for her, that had happened a few years prior and she enjoyed the dollars she brought in.

Stephanie also made sure to mention that Alice was a tough but fair boss. She didn't let customers take advantage of her employees, male and female. To her, it was a business, and she ran a clean one. As long as I worked my scheduled shifts and kept my nose clean, Alice would keep me on the payroll. She had also explained that Alice's club didn't allow the dancers to strip completely down. She had a thong and panty rule that she was very strict about.

I had been so nervous about taking the stage for Alice that day last week; it wasn't often that I found myself the center of attention willingly. But she had made sure that I felt at ease as I suggested a song to dance to.

The moment I took the stage, lights had illuminated the apron and I could no longer see the tables lining the floor. My heart had been pounding in my chest, but when the first chords of the rock song had filled the room, my tension had fallen away. My parents hadn't had much extra money growing up for me to do all of the fun things most children did. Extra sports, field trips, and vacations? Those were off the table. But my mother had put me in dance class the moment I learned to walk. I was skilled in ballet, jazz, tap, pretty much any form of dance I could find myself in. She had worked overtime to help afford the classes.

But when she died, I had stopped dancing. My heart was no longer in it. Dancing had been something that I did to make her proud but without her smiling face in the audience for every recital and practice, I found that dancing no longer held any appeal.

I also worried that my father would suffer in agony watching me do something that would remind him of my mother.

But when I took the stage, all of it came back. Every movement, every sashay, every toe kick. I felt nothing but the music as it pulsed around me.

Before that day, I had never stepped inside a strip club and I was certain that I had found myself in what someone would call an upscale gentlemen's club. I wasn't naïve enough to know that there weren't seedier clubs where I could have found myself.

Alice had clapped after my performance and I was surprised by her praise before doing my best to school my features. Thankfully she hired me on a trial period giving me a more than generous salary and explained that tips and cash left on stage would be mine as well. I had asked what the typical dancer made each night and she shrugged her shoulders, saying that it wasn't her business.

Stephanie had filled in that blank by saying that she easily brought home around two thousand dollars on a slow night. That would quickly help cover my expenses and my tuition if I did my best.

My first night dancing was tonight and I was both nervous and excited. I'm sure my nerves would rattle my bones until I actually took the stage, but I knew that my hands were tied if I wanted to stay at Wellington.

Finishing my run, I hopped in the shower then threw on an oversized T-shirt and shorts before heading toward the animal shelter to see my friend Jolee. She was in charge of the fundraiser at the local animal shelter where she volunteered all of her free time.

If there was anyone that had a heart of gold, it was Jolee. We had met in a general education class last year and had quickly formed a friendship as newbies at the school. The two of us and Keeley stuck out like sore thumbs amongst all of the other well-off students.

Ford had been in our class and spent the majority of the time antagonizing Jolee until one day, they showed up as a couple. The rest was history.

Jolee and I didn't get to spend much time together outside of classes, but I hoped that would change once I was able to move into my new apartment in her building.

Walking the few blocks to the shelter, I was surprised at the growing crowd out on the lawn. From Jolee's text yesterday, it didn't seem like the event was supposed to start for another few hours. As I got closer, I noticed a group of guys moving carnival-like equipment around.

The Ridge Rogues.

It was unfair to have that many good-looking guys in one area. I didn't know much about them, except they were all adoptive brothers. Their mother, Dr. Fincher, was a professor at the university and had adopted all of the troubled boys before her husband had passed away a few years ago.

The rumors about the boys traveled far and wide around campus. Even the one still in high school had his name mentioned a time or two. I didn't believe most of what was said, liking to form opinions about people on my own. Exceptions could always be made, though, and I had learned that there was always some sort of truth to a rumor.

I knew of Ford, who stood in the mass of guys looking like the broody male that he was. If I hadn't known that he loved Jolee so much, he would be the first one I'd stand clear of. He gave off a vibe that threatened anyone that got too close. All those days and weeks of being on the receiving end of his hatred must have taken a toll on Jolee.

Link, the eldest of the brothers, stood back with his muscular arms crossed against his chest. He walked around campus with an air about him that said he was better than everyone else. Once he had substituted for another graduate student in my economy class and I was pretty sure not a single female remembered anything he discussed in class, their hormones blocking any information to their brain. He reminded me of royalty with his dark blond hair neatly tied back behind his head and his neatly pressed dress clothes, even though he was outside working on setting up the fundraiser.

Recognition alluded me as I stared at three of the other guys, all varying in age. One I vaguely recognized as a player on the baseball team, but the other two I had never seen on campus before.

Off on the side, I noticed Jolee directing some people where to place a dunk tank while a small fenced-in area had a bunch of puppies yipping for her attention. Something must have caught her eye because she glanced in my direction, waving at someone past me before she noticed me standing in her peripheral.

"Sarah!" she called out, waving me closer as she finished directing the dunk tank placement.

"Hey, this looks great. You are definitely going to have a big crowd today. The weather is perfect too."

"I'm really hoping everything goes okay. It was so nice for all of these vendors to donate to the fundraiser. Of course, I'm also hoping we find a few families to adopt some of the animals."

"You know I'd take as many as I could, if I could." I had begged my parents growing up for a pet, even something as small as a fish, but pets were an expense that my family couldn't afford. I understood, especially as I got older and realized how much having a pet would cost just in food. But it never stopped my yearning to come home to something that loved me as much as I loved it. "Maybe one day," I added. With the new job, I could give thought to adopting a dog or cat. I wasn't picky. Though the small beagle mix that was howling to get Jolee's attention definitely caught my eye.

"I'm so glad you could make it and help out today."

"You know that I wouldn't miss it. I'm sorry I can't stay for very long. Tonight is my first night on the stage and I want to rest up," I told her, watching as Jolee's eyes grew double their size.

She gripped my arm and pulled me to the side, using the building to block us from everyone on the front lawn.

"Are you sure that you are comfortable doing this? You know that I would try to help you out. I could ask Willow." Her concern for me was palpable, but I didn't want the pity. I knew what I was doing, and I was prepared for the consequences, whatever they may be. Even my father understood when I told him how I planned to get the funds. He had been upset at first, but when I assured him that Alice treated her employees with respect, he seemed to be a bit more at ease. I wanted Jolee to understand as well. This was how I was going to be able to stay at school.

"I'm fine. I promise it's not what you're imagining. It's classier than I thought and my boss is great, so are the other dancers."

"But stripping, Sarah? It just doesn't seem like you, that's all."

Anger bubbled up under my skin at her accusation and I had to work hard to squash the feeling. She meant well and I understood what she was trying to say. I was just an average-looking girl behind my baggy clothes and ball cap that hid behind my surroundings, preferring to hide in the shadows. Dancing tonight would put me front and center with a spotlight that would follow my every move.

"I'm coming off as a bitch," she added as she shook her head, gazing down at the ground. "I think it's great that you're doing whatever you can to make money to stay in school. It's admirable, Sarah."

"I feel like everyone would do the same if they were in my situation."

She shook her head, strands of her wavy brown hair caressing her cheeks.

"No, they wouldn't, Sarah. Most would head home without a backward glance."

I thought she was wrong. It seemed to me that most people would do whatever they could to achieve their dreams, even strip to make money to pay for their school's tuition.

Wanting to change the subject, I asked Jolee what she needed me to do to finish helping to set up the fundraiser. She directed me to the small kitchen inside the building to gather the bottles of water and place them in the large coolers sporadically placed around the lawn.

An hour later, a food truck arrived just as the fundraiser was slated to begin. Local news crews, including the university paper, were mingling around the property and I was doing my best to stay away from them all.

On the other hand, the Ridge Rogues were hamming it up for the camera, all except the eldest one. Bending down to refill one of the coolers with bottles of water, I glanced by the dunk tank to find the same guy that had laughed at me the week before when I had tripped on campus. He was extremely attractive, with his hair falling across his face in a way that seemed both deliberate and a mistake at the same time. It was no wonder almost all of the news crews were surrounding him; she was certain that the camera would love him, just like the gaggle of women waiting for him to take his turn at the tank.

I couldn't deny that I wasn't the slightest bit tempted to watch him strip off his shirt and take his place in the acrylic tube. Even from afar, I could see how well he filled out his white T-shirt and lime green swimming trunks. The shorts would look ridiculous on just about anyone else, but not him.

"Hey," a deep voice said from beside me, and I startled, causing the lid of the cooler to fall down onto my fingertips.

"Ouch!" I cried out after prying my fingers free from the plastic lid.

"Sorry!" the newcomer said as he took a step closer to me while I cradled my hand against my chest. "I didn't mean to scare you. I just wanted to grab a bottle of water."

"It's okay. I was lost in my own world," I explained as I turned my attention to him. I recognized him from one of my classes, but I couldn't remember his name to save my life.

"I'm Trey. You were in my business ethics class, right?"

"Yeah, I think so. I'm Sarah," I replied as I reached out with my injured hand to shake his.

As he reached for a bottle of water, I took in his thin but muscular frame. He was built like a swimmer or a runner with lean muscles and a trim waist. As he stood back up, I did my best to hide the fact that I had been checking him out, but I knew I was failing since I could feel the blush rising on my pale cheeks.

"Are you here for business or pleasure?"

"Excuse me?" I didn't understand what he meant and cocked my head to the side.

"I just meant, are you here for the fun or to adopt?"

"Oh, well. . . my friend Jolee is the one that organized the fundraiser. I'm just here to help and support her."

"Hm. . . that's very friendly of you. Maybe I can show you some fun later?"

If it wasn't for the cocky smile he was sending in my direction, I would have thought he meant to enjoy the festivities. But it seemed like the only festivities he planned to enjoy were the kind that took place in his bed.

"Um. . .thanks for the offer, but I need to stay and help clean up when the fundraiser is over."

"That's a shame. Maybe another time," he said before turning around and heading toward a group of women that were petting the puppies.

I'm not sure why I was surprised to find his attention so easily moving on to someone else. Hadn't I witnessed it time and time again that I wasn't pretty enough or interesting enough to hold a man's attention? At least, that was what my high school ex had said. My attempt at relationships ended there. I had no time for them anyway.

Ignoring the pang of hurt in my chest I headed back to the kitchen to fill the coolers with the last bottles of water. Keeping my mind on a task helped me forget about what I had to do that evening. I wondered what Trey would think if he saw me dancing instead of the shimmy of pain he witnessed.

Finishing the task Jolee assigned, I went in search of her until the smell from the food truck assaulted me. The charred burgers and salted French fries caused my stomach to growl loudly. It took just a few minutes before I found myself moving briskly to join the line.

I should have known that even waiting in line for some lunch would be eventful. Just as I approached the end of the line, I tripped on my own feet. The movement

caused me to fall into the man that would be ahead of me
in line.

"I'm sorry," I whispered as I tried to tuck my chin
against my chest, shrinking myself against the onslaught
of hate-filled words that I expected to come. I had learned
many times before that people, in general, didn't like to
be run into. Especially the boys at Wellington University.

At first, I didn't notice whose back I had slammed
into, but as he turned around, I peered up beneath my
lashes and was astonished to come face to face with the
Ridge Rogue that had laughed at me a week ago. Why
couldn't he be neck-deep in the dunk tank instead of
standing before me as I embarrass myself again?

His green eyes bore into mine and I was bracing
for him to lash out at me. Instead, he fell silent, his tanned
skin growing ashen by the second as he stared at me. I
wasn't sure what he was seeing as he looked me over, but
his eyes showed fear as if he had seen a ghost.

I couldn't pull my eyes away from his as we stood
in silence. It wasn't until Jolee approached that the spell
we were in seemed to be broken. She was barely able to
say hello before the man in question dashed away,
leaving a trail of confusion in his wake.

"What just happened?" Jolee asked as my eyes followed his retreating back.

"I literally tripped and fell into him by accident, and then he stormed off."

"Really?"

I didn't bother responding to Jolee; instead, I let the worrisome feeling crawl up my spine until it threatened to drown me. His reaction left me on edge. Sure, I wasn't the most attractive thing to find when you turned around after being bumped into, but I had apologized, nor had I fallen into him on purpose.

"It was just another clumsy moment for me."

"It's just. . .Archer is such a laid-back kind of guy. I've never seen that expression on him before."

It was a relief to know that I wasn't the only one that noticed his expression change. When he initially turned around, it seemed as if he was merely slightly annoyed at my collision with his muscular frame, but his entire demeanor had changed once his gaze settled on my face.

"I'm not sure what happened, but it was like he was looking right through me."

The feeling of his haunted gaze was going to stay with me for a while. I could still sense it on my skin and it left me uneasy.

"I'm sorry. Maybe I startled him? Anyway, I came over to see if you wanted to join us for dinner tomorrow. I figured since you'll be moving into your new place that we could help welcome you to the complex."

"That sounds nice. Can I bring anything?" I asked her as we took a few steps closer to the food truck. My stomach growled loudly as the smells of the fried food grew stronger.

"No need. It's Chance's turn for food, so that means it's either pizza or spaghetti. Are you sure you don't want any help moving? I have access to six strapping men that I can convince to help," she said with a laugh.

"Honestly, I have an air mattress, television, and suitcases. I think I can handle it, but I do appreciate the offer."

"Alright, well, thank you again for your help today and good luck tonight. I kind of wish that I could come watch, but I don't want to make you uncomfortable."

Jolee was right in that assumption, but maybe once I felt more comfortable, I could invite her to watch a dance or two. I wasn't embarrassed about my body; I'd been a fan of running and yoga for as long as I could remember. My fear stemmed from having everyone's eyes on me.

"Maybe once I get settled, you could come to watch."

"Sounds like a plan. I'll let you enjoy your lunch. Call me tomorrow if you end up needing help." Resting her hand gently on my arm, she drew my attention away from the food truck's chalkboard menu and back onto her. "And don't let Archer's reaction bother you. I'm sure it was nothing."

I was sure that it was something more than nothing, and as I made my way to work that night, the look in his green eyes seemed to haunt me until they were all that I could see. If there was one night where I didn't need a distraction, it was this one. But all that I could do was close my eyes, take a deep breath, and dance like my life depended on it. Because right now, it did.

RENEE HARLESS

CHAPTER THREE

ARCHER

The spring sun was shining brightly in Boston this morning, melting the last bit of winter's snow. I was up early to help my brother, Ford, and his girlfriend, Jolee, set up a fundraiser at the local animal shelter down the road from Wellington University. This was where she had volunteered her time outside of classes and her job at the veterinary clinic. I didn't know how she found the time or energy to do any of this – she amazed not only me but all of the Ridge Rogues.

"Hey, where do you want this?" I asked Jolee as I carried the parts of the dunk tank. She had asked us all to volunteer our time this Saturday without any qualms, mainly because she knew we would say yes. For how she was able to save our brother Ford from himself, we would do whatever she wanted. Plus, we all loved animals and the cause.

"Over by the big oak tree." She pointed in the direction she wanted across the front lawn.

I carried the large contraption over to the oak tree and sat it in the shade. People were already starting to arrive just as the workers at the shelter began carrying some of the dogs outside. They were the ones eligible for adoption. Ford was going to have his hands full trying to keep Jolee from bringing another pet home – they were still working on house training their puppy Balboa.

Glancing around the yard, I noticed a hose tucked around the side and went to grab it to start filling the dunk tank. Ford struggled to carry a few blowers for the bounce house and inflatable slides, and I was very tempted to turn the hose on him but held myself back. I didn't need Jolee coming after me. She may be beautiful, but she had a vicious tongue.

By lunchtime, the parking lot was filled and there were lines of students waiting to dunk volunteers in the tank or wait for food from a local food truck.

Knowing that my chance to grab a bite to eat was shrinking by the second, I made my way to the food truck and waited in line, pulling the brim of my hat down low. I was tired from the week before. My most recent conquest making more out of our two nights together than I ever promised her. She was showing up everywhere I turned and I knew that I was going to have to lay things out more clearly for her.

Behind me, a soft voice rang out as she bumped into my back. "I'm sorry."

I turned around to tell her that it was fine, but my tongue caught in my throat. Her red hair hung down in soft waves around her face and her pale skin shone under the sun. But it was her brown eyes that held me captive. They reminded me of someone so familiar, someone I hadn't thought of for over ten years. The woman reached out to touch me and then suddenly I was transported back in time.

I shivered in the cold, dank apartment. The walls were peeling away and the floor felt wet beneath my feet. I sat on the couch, one of the springs poking into my thigh as I held tightly to the only picture we had of my parents.

The phone in the kitchen kept ringing, but I was scared to answer it. I was afraid it was my teacher calling to yell at me again. She didn't like how I acted in school and how I never turned in any homework, but I didn't have anyone to help me.

My parents left for a trip one day and never came back, my sister, Natalie, told me that they went to be with the angels. She packed me up in the small car my mother used and we moved into this nasty apartment that smelled like old people.

I hadn't seen my sister in three days and I hadn't left the apartment to go to school because I was afraid I wouldn't have a place to come back to.

Just as the phone stopped ringing, my sister stumbled into the apartment. I rushed to her and wrapped myself around her legs, but she kicked me away. Her red hair that had reminded me of Clifford the Dog had turned a weird color since my parents left, it was more like straw now. I didn't like it. I didn't like how her arms had bruises all over them, either.

"Sissy?" I asked as I scrambled onto my feet. My stomach had been growling for two days and all I had to eat was cereal. I hoped that she came home with more food because we didn't have anything left.

My sister bypassed me and went to the room we shared, ignoring me completely, as she slammed the door closed.

I counted as high as I could before I knocked on the door again, but my sister didn't answer.

"Natalie?" I called out as I peeked through a crack in the door.

She was draped halfway on the bed and halfway off like I did when I was dreaming about fighting bad guys.

"Sissy?" I said as I walked closer to her and rocked her shoulder with my hand. Usually, she would move or try to shove me away, but she didn't do any of those things.

"Sissy, wake up. My school keeps calling and I'm hungry."

I repeated the same motion until I rocked her so hard that she fell off the bed.

But she didn't do anything. She just laid there.

I knew what that meant. I had seen it on television when Natalie had stayed out late one night.

"Sissy!!!!!"

"Oh. . .um. . ," she murmured, breaking me free from my flashback.

I was glad that she had taken two large steps back because I was completely disgusted with myself and needed to find an escape.

"Hey, guys," Jolee said as she approached.

"I'm sorry, but I need to go," I told her without a backward glance.

And I just prayed that I didn't run into anyone as I sprinted home to burn my skin under the hot water.

It had been years since I had felt this dirty, this unglued. Leave it to a gorgeous redhead to bring my haunted past into the present.

I lost the contents of my stomach the first time in the bushes that lined the University's outskirt sidewalk. The second time I barely made it into my apartment and to the hall bath before I collapsed onto the cool tile floor. I was grateful that Jolee had been living with us at that moment because I knew the floor and bathroom were clean. Getting sick in a dirty bathroom wasn't my favorite thing to do and I had experienced it more than once as a kid and an adult.

Closing my eyes, I found myself murmuring the Lord's name as the eyes of the woman that had run into me immediately sprang in my mind. I had seen her around campus before, but had no idea who she was. All I knew was that she hid behind oversized clothes that were two or three sizes larger than her body. Before today I had thought that there was nothing remarkable about her or her face. She was pretty in the girl next door sort of way, nothing remarkable or any features that stood out. If it wasn't for the red hair and large brown doe eyes, I wouldn't have looked twice at her.

"Shit," I groaned as I recalled the last time I had seen my sister when she was clean. Her hair and eyes had been almost the same color and shade as the girl that had jostled me. Drug use and prostitution had morphed my sister into someone I had no longer recognized. Even now, I wasn't sure why being that close to the red-haired woman triggered a memory from my past that I had compartmentalized and stowed away back into the depths of my memory.

I wasn't sure how long I had laid on the cold floor, but I was startled at the sound of the apartment door slamming, which rattled the bathroom wall.

"Archer?" a voice called out and I recognized it as Ford's, which meant Jolee wouldn't be far behind.

Standing, I stood in front of the sink and glanced at myself in the mirror. My eyes appeared lifeless and troubled, just like they had been when I was found in my sister's apartment cold and hungry. Splashing cold water onto my face, I tried to bring life back into my features, but it did very little.

Suddenly I was exhausted as I stepped out of the bathroom to find Ford standing in the kitchen holding two bottles of water. My body felt drained and I wanted nothing more than to climb into my bed and sleep for days. Except I knew that sleep would allude me.

"There you are. Jolee asked me to check in with you. Said you left the fundraiser in a hurry."

It was moments like this that I hated having so many people watching out for me. No one other than our mother knew the extent of what I had gone through as a child, each of us keeping our experiences locked away. We had only recently learned of Ford's past when his father threatened Jolee.

"Yeah, I didn't mean to leave her high and dry like that. I just. . .forgot that I had something to do," I said, but I could see that Ford didn't believe me. He cocked a brow in my direction as he silently handed me a bottle of water. Untwisting the top, I gulped down the chilled liquid, the water soothing my scratchy throat.

"You know that I don't believe you, right?"

"Yep."

"But you, ugh, know that you can talk to Jolee or me, right?"

"Yep."

"Going to say anything else?" he asked, annoyed with my one-word answers.

"Nope."

"Alright, at least tell Jolee I tried, okay? She has a soft spot for you. God only knows why."

"Because I'm charming, attractive, and have a great personality?"

"Conceited much?" he said as he brushed past me to make his way to his room.

"Just stating the facts."

The door to Ford's room closed with a flourish and I stood in a haze for a moment staring at the large piece of wood. As tired as I felt, my body was itching to feel something – anything. Grabbing my phone from my back pocket, I dialed up the number for my friend Trey and messaged him asking if he wanted to hit up one of the bars close to campus. There was never any shortage of women vying for a spot in my bed or for me to warm theirs; so long as they understood it would never amount to a relationship, I had no problem losing myself in a night with a stranger.

***

My breath was shallow, barely able to fill my lungs with much-needed oxygen. I kept relieving the horror of finding my sister's lifeless body lying on her bed. My nightmare began the day she died, trying to fend for myself as a ten-year-old without letting any of our neighbors know that she had passed away. I was afraid of what would happen to me, of where I would go.

It took only three days for someone to pound on the apartment door. The landlord wanted his rent payment and he was tired of waiting. I had just returned from school for the day to find the landlord letting himself into the apartment. On my feeble legs, I ran as fast as I could and launched myself at him, knocking him off balance. In his attempt to right himself, he fell into the bedroom door where my sister slept.

The smell was rancid. Even in my dreams, I could remember the putrid scent. The landlord had thrown up all over the white shag rug that my sister had loved, which broke something in me. Even as small as I had been, I had pounded the guy's back for ruining something my sister had loved.

When the police arrived, I was scared and outraged. I remember the officer telling CPS that I was like a caged animal, ready to lash out at anyone that came close. I'm not sure how they had expected me to act, but losing your sister and only living relative to drugs was not something I figured most people would take lightly.

I arrived at the club half out of my mind as it were and I immediately sidled up to the bar to get my signature vodka tonic. Over in the dimly lit corner, I found Trey surrounded by a gathering of women as he stood with a pool stick, obviously waiting for me to arrive and join him in a game.

"Hey, man," he called out when he noticed my approach. He never minded when I joined him on a lady hunt, mainly because he enjoyed being my wingman and having his pick of whatever females I turned down.

"Hey, Trey. Who do we have here?" I asked the group, but my attention was on the closest woman with platinum blonde hair. She was barely wearing any clothing, just enough to cover the important parts that I planned to explore later, and she was wearing enough makeup to fill a drug store, but she would easily do for the night.

The woman must have sensed my interest in her because she moved herself closer until she could possessively place her hand on my arm, staking her claim.

Trey introduced the rest of the girls, but my new companion whispered in my ear that her name was Callie and she wasn't wearing any panties.

The last bit was information that I would keep tucked in the back of my mind. She would be easy enough to take home so long as I made sure she didn't get drunk. That was the one rule in the game I played: the woman had to be of sound mind. If she was under any influence, she wouldn't comprehend it when I explained that it was a one-time thing. More than once, the women were convinced that I had made promises to them.

When in fact, I never *ever* made promises.

"Ready to play?" I asked Trey as I grabbed a pool stick while he began setting up the balls.

"Let's go."

With my arm around Callie's waist, I whispered in her ear that I would win the game for her tonight and she promptly giggled, the response that I had hoped for.

It didn't take long for a crowd to grow around us as it usually did. Trey and I played pool together since we ended up in the same foster home when we were fifteen. I didn't last long in that home, due to my attitude and anger issues, but I had stayed in touch with Trey. I had even helped him get financial assistance to come to Wellington Ridge.

By the end of our third game, Trey and I had a nice buzz and I was more than ready to head back to my apartment with my guest.

"Ready to go, sweetheart?" I whispered in her ear, watching as she tried to smile seductively but her lips pulled in oddly. It was obvious that she'd had lip injections already. A bit young for surgery but I didn't mind. I could only imagine what those lips would look like wrapped around my cock later.

She played coy as she fake argued with her friends about leaving with a stranger. It was a routine that I was all too familiar with. The women I met at bars, especially if they were there with a group of their friends, would always make it seem like they were putting their friends out until they could be convinced to "go home with that hot guy."

Just as expected, Callie wrapped her friends in a vicious hug and promised to text when she arrived at my apartment. I rolled my eyes at Trey, who was witness to the routine on more than one occasion as well.

"I'm ready now. How far away is your place?" she asked, stumbling from the bar as she teetered on her high heels. I had watched her meticulously to make sure that she didn't drink too much and knew that she had only drunk two red-colored drinks served in a martini glass. I assumed that they were cosmos and had very little alcohol content. Callie was putting on a show and I was willing to play along.

"I'm three blocks away. Close enough to walk."

She pouted, realizing that she was going to have to skip a ride share service and walk precariously on her heels. That wasn't my problem.

"Don't worry. It will be worth it," I told her as I reached around her waist and gripped a globe of her ass in my hand. It was firm enough that I was going to have fun with her tonight. I bet she'd like a bit of spanking.

"Oh, I bet it will be."

As we approached the complex, I turned toward Callie and gave her my signature smile. The one that I knew landed me the deal every time. The one that made women crazy and convinced them that they were making a good decision. This was all a power play for me. I wasn't taking advantage of what they were offering, but I made sure that they knew that there was nothing more than this one night, this one play.

"It's just for tonight, okay? I don't want you to expect sunshine and rainbows in the morning."

Callie nodded as she leaned forward, trying to seal her lips against mine. I quickly turned my head away. Kissing wasn't part of the plan either. Luckily most of the women I brought home forgot about that part of intimacy when I put my hands on them.

"I'm ready for you, Archer," she purred, her lips rubbing against the shell of my ear.

Grabbing her hand that was slithering up my chest, I tugged her behind me as I entered the building and moved toward the third floor.

Jolee and Ford were cuddled on the couch when we entered and I tried to slink past them without receiving their condescending glare, which was downright hypocritical from Ford, who used to play the same games I did. Instead, I caught Jolee's eyes and she shook her head before turning back to whatever they were watching on television.

"Hi, I'm Callie!" my partner said as she giggled and I yanked a bit harshly on her hand to have her follow me to my room across the way.

"Don't talk to my friends," I growled as I shut the door and locked it. "Now, let's get started."

CHAPTER FOUR

SARAH

S tanding in the open space, I measured the distance from one wall to the other, noting how much furniture I could possibly fit in the studio. The room was small, just enough for a bed and probably a couch and table, but I was determined to make the space feel as homey as I could.

During my walk-through this morning, I checked out the updated bathroom and was surprised to find new tile, shower, sink, and toilet. The landlord explained that the previous tenant had destroyed everything when he left. It was unfortunate for him, but it was definitely a gain for me. Using a bathroom that someone else had once used always sort of freaked me out.

The kitchen was small, with just a few cabinets, a sink, and appliances, but I didn't need much room for storage.

Turning in a circle to take in the entire space, I raised my arms above my head and stretched. My bones and muscles ached in places that I didn't know could ache. My first night on stage had started off less than stellar. The music didn't sync correctly and I had tripped as I walked on stage, but after that fiasco, the rest of the evening had gone well. I danced four times on the stage and then did one private dance. I made more cash with the private dance than I ever would have expected and I hoped that Alice would let me do more of them.

When she had told me that I had been requested for a private session, I had panicked. I had no idea what to expect, but she explained that there was a no-touch rule and a bouncer was located in each room. That knowledge set me at ease and I easily earned the eight hundred dollars that the older man had paid me.

Overall I came home with roughly two thousand dollars and a newfound respect for the women working at Phoenix's Fire. Not only were they supporting themselves, but they were in great shape. I worked out daily, but I had put myself through the wringer working just one night.

Luckily, I wasn't scheduled to work again until Tuesday and Thursday. If I could continue to make money like I had made last night, or at least close to it, I should be able to cover my tuition before the due date.

As much as I wanted to pass out and sleep for the next few hours, I needed to go buy a bed and look around some thrift stores for furniture. Grabbing my phone, I sent a message to Jolee asking if she wanted to join me on a shopping trip. She responded quickly and said that she would be down in a couple of minutes. That gave me just enough time to grab a granola bar and a bottle of water. That was another stop that I needed to make; I needed to get groceries.

I had just opened my suitcase and began hanging a few of the clothes when a knock on my door sounded.

"Come in!" I called out without checking the peephole, but I knew Jolee was coming over.

"You should really lock your door, Sarah." Jolee was very strict about safety after she was assaulted on campus as she exited the library last year. She was lucky that Link, one of the Ridge Rogues, had been passing through and fought off her assailants.

"I know. I'm sorry. I'll be better about it."

"So, this is it?" she asked as she took in the space, flitting over to the bathroom and kitchen to give them a once-over.

"This is it."

"I love it. The landlord did a great job remodeling the bathroom. I'm glad you were able to find a space here in the complex. I like having you close by."

"Me too. I'm just glad that the rent isn't outrageous."

Hooking the hanger on the tension rod in the closet, I turned to find Jolee inspecting me, her eyes trailing up and down my body in concern.

"How did it go last night?" she asked.

"It was good. Actually, it was great. I made way more than I thought and I was even booked for a private show."

"Private?" she questioned in alarm. "Is that safe? I mean, this just seems so unlike you, Sarah."

"I preferred it to the stage. And there was a bouncer in the room with me so he enforced the no-touching rule.

"I know that it's hard to imagine me dancing for money, but it's something I need to do to make ends meet right now. And I love to dance. It's been nice to get back into it again."

"I know and I realize that I'm being small-minded about the entire thing. I'm all for women's empowerment. I just don't want something bad to happen to you. Especially since you're riding public transportation to get home at that crazy hour."

Walking over to Jolee, I wrapped her in my arms and comforted her as best as I could. She was a concerned friend and I had no reason to be upset with her reaction. It wasn't much different than my father's had been.

"I'm fine, Jolee. Sometimes we have to do unpleasant things to reach our dreams. And I promise, Alice, my boss, really does take care of her employees. Our safety is her top priority.

"Anyway, what kind of shopping do we have in store?"

"Well, I don't know if you can tell, but I need a bit of everything. I'm thinking mostly some thrifts shops that I found close by and Target for some bedding and kitchenware."

"What about a bed?"

"I ordered one online a couple of days ago. It should be delivered tomorrow. I'll just sleep with some blankets tonight."

"Okay. Chance is letting us borrow his truck, so we'll be able to haul everything back, and hopefully, they'll help us unload."

"I can pay them in beer."

Jolee swirled the set of keys around her fingers as she chuckled. "They will definitely accept that offer."

As we left the complex, heading toward the spot where Chance's truck was parked, we overheard some shouting and I noticed Jolee's frame instantly grow rigid. Leaning toward me, she whispered that it was Archer arguing with his guest. My first instinct was to roll my eyes.

"But. . .but I made you breakfast," the woman whined.

"I never asked you to. I told you that it was just one night," Archer replied in a tone that sounded as if he been in the same scenario before.

"But I thought things were different last night."

"See this is what I'm talking about. You're already suffocating me." His voice seemed distant as if he was moving away from the woman.

"I'm sorry! I'm sorry!" the woman shouted at him, the sound of her feet pounding on the asphalt had me believing that she was chasing after Archer."I didn't mean to mess everything up. Please give me another chance."

They had moved far enough away that I could no longer make out their conversation, but I looked over to Jolee as she climbed into the driver's side of the truck and sensed that this wasn't the first time she overheard a similar conversation like that with Archer.

"That happen often?" I asked as I joined her in the truck.

"More often than it should. I don't know what kind of web that boy spins, but no matter how domineering and assholey he comes across, the women he brings home always end up thinking that he doesn't want anything more because of something that they did. I can't figure it out."

As we drove to the first thrift store, I thought about what Jolee had said. It made me think that Archer was more despicable than I originally imagined. It was one thing to laugh at me as I tripped on campus or to run away when you find me standing behind you in line. But to manipulate women on purpose? That seemed like the lowest of lows.

Hours later, Jolee and I hefted a mid-century modern credenza that had seen better days into the bed of the truck. We'd already scored some secondhand bedroom and living room furniture, but when I saw this piece resting on the corner of a residential street, I knew that I needed to grab it. I had visions of sanding down the piece and giving it new life.

"Wow, I can't believe someone was getting rid of this," I said with excitement, even though I could tell that Jolee was less than enthused. She had called most of the items I picked up junk. "We still need to stop by Target so that I can grab sheets, kitchenware, and some food." Glancing over my shoulder as I stepped up into the truck, I asked Jolee, "Do you think someone will try to take the things in the back if we go now?"

Jolee laughed a full-belly cackle at my question. By the time her laughter subsided, she had tears streaming down her red cheeks. I didn't think it was all that funny.

"No, I can say with absolution that I don't think anyone is going to take your haul."

"If you say so."

"I do. I really do. Let me go ahead and text Ford so that the guys can be ready in an hour or so to help us load these into your apartment. Are there any other stops we need to make after Target?"

I thought about all the things I needed to get to turn the trash into treasure. "Probably a stop at the hardware store, but I can go later today."

"Might as well go while we're out."

Two hours later, I hefted two of the couch cushions under my arms as I followed Ford, Chase, Rylan, and Link up the stairs to my apartment. I was secretly glad that Archer wasn't here to help. I wasn't so sure that I could keep my comments to myself after what I witnessed this morning.

Once all of the furniture was stacked in the center of the room I thanked the guys with a case of beer for each of them, Jolee letting me know their favorite brands ahead of time.

"Are you joining us for dinner?" Jolee asked and the guys readily agreed.

Chase chimed in before I could respond. "It's my night to cook, which means I'm ordering pizza, which will go great with the beer you provided."

Remembering that I agreed to Jolee's invite at the fundraiser, I said, "I'm in. Thanks for the invite."

A few minutes later, they piled out of my apartment, leaving me by myself with the piles of furniture that I needed to put my mark on. I may have had an addiction to do-it-yourself shows and I had convinced myself that I could tackle these projects.

Unpacking the orbital sander I had purchased at the hardware store, I set my mind on the credenza that Jolee sneered at. I was determined to transform this piece just as I planned on transforming myself.

Since I had already provided the booze for tonight's dinner at Ford's apartment he shared with some of his brothers, I wasn't sure what to bring. While I was on the phone with my weekly check in with my dad, I asked him for his garlic knot recipe. Luckily, I grabbed all of the ingredients at the market across the street and baked the doughy goodness while I finished sanding the credenza.

I had lost track of time and when the alarm on my phone sounded, I didn't even have time to take a shower. I figured since the guys had already seen me in my typical oversized T-shirt and cut-off denim shorts, I didn't need to worry about impressing them further.

Standing in the bathroom over the tub, I tugged my hair free from the ponytail and shook the dust from the strands. Looking in the mirror, I sighed, knowing that this was as good as it was going to get as I brushed a few more clumps of dust from the front strands.

Grabbing the plastic container filled with the garlic knots, I left my apartment and headed toward Ford's. I knocked on the door expecting one of the guys from earlier to answer, but I was surprised when Archer was the one to open the door. His face grimaced as he appraised me. I knew I didn't come close to what he had planned to find on the other side of the door.

Archer began to close the door without a word until I finally spoke up and murmured Jolee's name.

"What?" he asked, halting his movements.

"I'm here for Jolee."

"Wait here," he said, slamming the door in my face. I wasn't sure what was going on, but I felt as rejected as the furniture I had picked up earlier that day.

A minute or two passed as I stood patiently outside the apartment door. Just as I was about to head back to my own apartment, the door opened, and Chance greeted me with a warm smile.

"Sorry about that, Sarah. Our douche brother has no manners." Chance ushered me inside and I offered him the container.

"Oh, what's this?" he asked as I followed him further into their large apartment.

"Homemade garlic knots," I explained as I entered the living area where everyone was congregated. All speaking stopped as Chance opened the container and seemed to sigh in delight.

"Fuck, you can join us for dinner every night if you can make more of these," he added as she shoved one of the doughy balls into his mouth.

In the blink of an eye, the rest of the brothers dove for the container and began fighting over the knots. I searched the room and found Jolee snickering in the corner as she played with her puppy Balboa.

"Come on, heathens. Let's eat," Jolee called out as she set her dog down and moved toward me, looping her arm through mine. "You can sit next to me," she added as she took me toward an oversized dining table.

I took the seat Jolee offered and she sat beside me while Ford carried bottles of beer to the table. The brothers began filling in the spare seats around the table just as Archer stepped out of the hallway. I had hoped that he would take one of the other open seats, but instead, I found him taking the one directly across from me.

I did my best not to look up at him, his gaze making me uncomfortable. Maybe it was the butterflies that took flight deep in my stomach when our eyes met in the hall or the fact that my heart raced as he locked his stare on me. None of the other brothers affected me the way that he did and I was growing increasingly uncomfortable.

Thankfully Chance broke the invisible tension across the table by asking me about my plans for the furniture and I quickly launched into the plans I had for them all. Even Link showed interest in the work I had already put into the credenza.

As we passed around a third box of pizza, I finally gathered the courage to look across the table at Archer and was surprised to find his eyes trained on me. There was a silent contest going on between us and I lost by breaking the stare first, but not before I noticed the smatterings of paint across his neck and a few on his forearms.

What could those be from?

He didn't seem like the artistic type or even the kind to get in a mishap with a paint can. But what did I know? He also didn't seem like the kind of guy that would be an asshole to a woman he shared the bed with. I was definitely learning how deceiving looks could be.

During the meal, he came across as the fun-loving brother that readily had a joke and a reason to make everyone laugh. But as I watched him closely, he could turn off the charm and happy-go-lucky nature in a split second. Just during dinner, I had watched his personality change no less than four times. And it completely fascinated me.

Once the gathering seemed to die down, I sat on the couch next to Jolee as we played with Balboa and the rest of the brothers lounged on the loveseat or the floor and watched a baseball game on television.

"So, what do you have in store for the rest of your summer?" Ford asked as he took the seat on the other side of Jolee. He had been in charge of cleaning up after dinner. I was certain he was glad that only pizza boxes and glass bottles would be tossed in the trash.

"Other than settling into the apartment, I'll probably look around for some volunteer work. If I weren't allergic to cats, I'd volunteer at the shelter with Jolee."

"You should check the bulletin board in the commons area by the coffee shop. They usually have a good list of places looking for volunteers," Ford pointed out.

"Thanks, I'll do that tomorrow."

My eyes traveled to the clock on the wall and I realized that I had probably worn out my welcome. I stood and thanked everyone for inviting me to dinner. Archer had retreated to his room after the meal, so I didn't have to worry about another awkward moment as I left.

As I reentered my apartment, I glanced at the pile of covers and blankets I had set up in the corner as my makeshift bed. I was certain that when I came back from dinner that exhaustion would take over my body. Instead, I found myself walking toward the credenza I had been working on and opened a can of paint. Sleep could wait.

CHAPTER FIVE

ARCHER

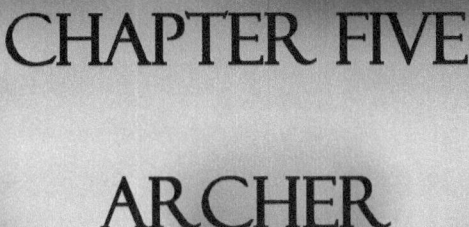

Paint splattered against the walls in my closet as I took my aggravation out on another crisp white canvas. Today I was feeling blues and greens. I painted without rhyme or reason, nor did I ever show anyone my work. It was just something that felt like an extension of me when I held a paint brush in my hand. It relaxed me in a way that exercise or drinking couldn't. And after the incident with Callie this morning, I had more than enough reasons to paint for the next couple of hours.

Callie was supposed to be another

in a long line of women that helped to keep my nightmares at bay. I was smart about the women that I brought home, but they were always a means to an end. I was able to wear myself out enough to fall into a dreamless sleep.

But the women always seemed to get the wrong idea. Granted, I had a few that were just as willing to spend a single night together, but the majority of the girls were students at the university and wanted to have the title of a Ridge Rogue's girlfriend. There was nothing that I could do or say that would change that desire for them. Jolee said that I needed to abstain from sex until I graduated, but she didn't know about the horrors that waited for me when I closed my eyes. I trusted my brothers enough not to share that information outside of our brotherhood. It was my past, my story, and I had no reason to share it with anyone else.

That had been what triggered my anger this morning with Callie. Normally I could easily let down my partner and send them on their way, always wondering where they had gone wrong, but Callie had been overly persistent in learning about me and my past. She had blabbered endlessly about her childhood and what brought her to Wellington and when she had paused for me to interject about my past, she was disappointed when I asked her to leave. When she took longer than I expected, I left the apartment and she readily followed, begging for forgiveness.

That was something that I wouldn't grant her even if she hadn't tried to pry into my past.

Grabbing another shade of blue, I smeared the paint onto the canvas until it resembled a wave in the oceanic image I was creating. The wave flowed but it wasn't perfect, cresting and breaking before it would reach the shore. I'd need to add white next to show the cap of the wave as it foamed and fell into itself.

My emotions felt like the wave I was painting after sitting through dinner. Jolee's friend joined us for pizza and I remembered her from the animal shelter fundraiser, but I couldn't remember her name. All that I knew was that she was a memory brought to life. My gaze was transfixed on her as she ate and laughed with my brothers and there was absolutely nothing that I could do to turn away. Even Jolee had kicked me under the table but I couldn't turn away. I was looking for something, anything, that would alert me that someone had sent this girl into my life as a reminder of my past.

I lost myself in the canvas as time ticked by, using the paint to rid myself of the awful memories popping up like daisies in a field. The chime on my phone sounded from my bedroom and I left my closet to find a text from Trey saying that Callie was spreading rumors at the bar we had been at the night before. It was nothing that I planned to worry about since it wasn't the first time someone lied about whatever relationship they thought that we had.

Falling across my bed, I turned my gaze to the canvases that lined the oversized closet I used as an art space. Most were crap that was now covered in blue splatters from my newest creation. I wasn't under any illusion that I had artistic talent. I simply enjoyed creating something from nothing.

I remembered Jolee's friend mentioning that she was working to fix up an old piece of furniture for her apartment. I wondered if she got the same enjoyment out of it as I did when I painted.

With no desire to join everyone out in the living room, I stayed hidden away and scrolled through my phone until the night sky descended through my window. The darkness drew me in and I fell asleep without having to lose myself in a strenuous activity. This time the image of red hair and large brown eyes flashed behind my lids until I woke up screaming, my voice hoarse and throat dry as I relived those turbulent times with my sister.

Knowing that I wasn't going to be able to fall back asleep, I made my way back to the closet and grabbed a clean white canvas. Earlier I had used blues and greens to try and calm my overactive mind, but now all I could see is red. Pools of blood-red and orange that would give way to the hell I was living in.

I woke the following day hunched over the easel with a paintbrush covered in red paint dangling from my hand. Arching my back, I stretched and tried to work the tired muscles, but it was no use. I knew better than to fall asleep while painting. I always ended up hurting worse than I would have if I had tolerated the nightmares.

Needing to fill my lungs with air, I quickly changed into a T-shirt and running shorts. As I exited the apartment, I noticed the rain coming down in sheets, the wind whipping the droplets around like they were nothing more than a feather. Most people didn't enjoy running in the rain, but it was my favorite. Not only did it keep me refreshed, but I never had to worry about someone else trailing along.

I made my way around the outskirts of the campus then followed the winding paths between each of the buildings. The school was empty for the most part during the summer breaks, though a few students still took classes that were offered in the summer session. I had taken a few the year before, which helped bring me closer to graduating.

Thunder sounded off in the distance and I knew it was a safe bet that a storm was approaching. I ducked inside the commons building and planned to spend some time there until the majority of the storm passed. At the small coffee shop, I ordered a drink and a muffin then tucked myself away at a corner table that gave me a view of the people coming and going from the building.

I was an observer by nature, much preferring to spend my time watching others than being watched. Though my behavior around campus said the opposite. I was the one that all of the guys on campus tried to emulate with my carefree attitude and easygoing lifestyle. They had no idea how rigid I was on the inside. How difficult it was to be someone that I wasn't. After being tossed around from foster home to foster home, I learned that if I wanted to stay somewhere and be cared for, I needed to be whatever they wanted. That theory applied to the students at Wellington Ridge as well. Ford had cornered the market on broody and closed off. I opted for open and approachable. So far, it had worked in my favor, but it was tiresome to be something for everyone else.

From the corner of my eye, a flash of red stole my attention from my internal musings. I watched the woman approach the bulletin board and scan the listings. While she was distracted, I took in her appearance. I could tell that beneath the shirt that was three sizes too big and shorts from the wrong decade, she had a body women would kill for. Today she wore a pair of black-rimmed glasses which hid the small freckles that dotted her cheeks. She wasn't unattractive, but she wasn't anything that made you do a double-take.

I continued to stare at her back as she scanned the pinned papers on the board. She ripped a few of the tags off listings and tucked them in the small purse she wore across her body. The woman didn't linger much longer before turning and exiting the building and walked into the storm raging outside.

Curiosity had me considering moving from my table and viewing the board to see what she may have been looking at, but luckily my limbs wouldn't comply.

My pocket vibrated and I almost jumped in my chair as it startled me. Reaching for my phone, I saw my adoptive mom's name flash on the screen.

"Hey, Mom," I greeted her.

"Hi, Archer. How are you?"

"Good. Just finished up a run."

"You always did love to play in the rain."

"Still do."

"Anyway, I was calling to see if you still planned on help with the Wellington Housing Alliance. We start the next build tomorrow."

"Yes, absolutely."

The Wellington Housing Alliance was a charity program that built houses for the less fortunate or those that may have lost their home due to a fire or natural disasters. All of the work was done by volunteers, and local businesses donated items inside the homes. I had been volunteering every summer with the WHA since I was sixteen and I looked forward to every home reveal.

"Okay. I'll be sure to add you to one of the groups."

"Thanks, Mom. Will I see you there?"

"I'm sure you will at some point. We're helping four families this summer. So I'll probably float between all the volunteer groups."

"Okay," I replied as I glanced out of the window and noticed that the rain had slowed to a steady drizzle. Silence followed on the other end of the call and I knew the question was coming before she even asked.

"Are you sleeping alright, Archer?" Dr. Tracy Fincher had been my advocate since I came into her care late in my teens. I had been listed as unadoptable but that hadn't stopped her and her husband from taking me in anyway. I had been in their care before, they were the first family I stayed with after I was found in my sister's apartment, but due to politics or whatever shit social services came up with, I had been moved to another foster family. Dr. Fincher was the one who had placed me in therapy to try and silence the nightmares, and it had worked for a short time, but they'd been coming back more and more frequently.

"I'm sleeping as well as I can."

"You let me know if we need to find another therapist, okay. No one should have to close their eyes and see the things that you did." Mom was horrified when she learned how many days I had lived on my own, even before my sister came home and lost her life. She did all that she could to try and help ease my burden.

"I've been painting again," I told her, knowing that she would be thrilled that I was actively pursuing my hobby again. I didn't dare tell her that it was how I stayed awake at night.

"Oh, Archer. That's wonderful news. I'd love to see a painting sometime."

"Maybe." She had been the first and only person I showed my artwork to. It was hard to hide when I lived in her house. But instead of ridiculing me as I had expected, she cheered me on. Honestly, Dr. Fincher was an angel.

"Well, I have some papers to get graded. I'm glad you're helping out the alliance again this year. It's such a wonderful cause. I'll see you tomorrow."

"Bye, Mom."

I took my time returning to my apartment, walking through the drizzle as if nature was my own personal shower. By the time I arrived, I was soaked to the bone again, and though it had been warm out for a Bostonian summer, I felt a chill down to my bones as I entered my bedroom. The painting from last night drew my eye in his vibrant red tones splattered haphazardly across the canvas. There was something familiar in the painting, something I couldn't quite put my finger on. A shiver traveled through my body as I continued to stare at my creation.

I just wasn't one-hundred percent sure that it was from the rain.

RENEE HARLESS

CHAPTER SIX

SARAH

I wasn't sure what to expect as I arrived at the location Dr. Fincher had directed me to via her email. While I was at the commons yesterday, I saw the volunteer sign-up sheet for the Wellington Housing Alliance. I tugged off the contact information for the program along with a few others, but it was my first choice. WHA was a program I had never heard of before, but after doing some diligent research, I had learned that they built homes around the town of Wellington for underprivileged families and those affected by natural disasters. All in all, it was a charitable organization headed by Dr. Fincher, one of the professors at Wellington Ridge University.

I wasn't enrolled in any of her classes, but the students seemed to love her even though she taught some of the most challenging courses on campus.

The surroundings were unfamiliar as I was deposited on the corner by the public transportation. If it weren't for the slew of construction equipment and a crowd of other volunteers, I would have worried that I was in the wrong place. Instead, I was greeted by a few classmates that I recognized as well as Dr. Fincher who was handing out cups of coffee to everyone as they arrived.

She quickly placed us in groups of ten that would work alongside a contractor and housing professionals. Pretty much, we were here to do the grunt work.

In each of the groups, she assigned one point person that would help direct the volunteers and keep them on task.

As Dr. Fincher joined our group to divvy out the assignments, she frowned as she called out Archer Calloway's name. I was certain that only one Archer attended Wellington and I knew from Ford that Dr. Fincher was his adoptive mother. The disappointment was etched on her face as she glanced around the gathering for her son.

"Well, I guess he is running late this morning. In the meantime, Sarah Hodges," she called out, and for some strange reason, I felt like a scolded child though I knew I had done nothing wrong.

"Yes, ma'am."

She looked up from her clipboard, eyes wide in surprise, then they quickly softened as she tried to hide her reaction to me. Something was up with these Ridge Rogues and their families if this is how they would all react to meeting me.

"I'm going to assign you as the leader this morning. Here is the task sheet for house three, which you all will be working on," she explained as she handed me a printed spreadsheet with a list of items that needed completion and the timeframes in which to complete. "I'm certain that we can handle this for today."

"Okay. Thank you, Dr. Fincher."

My group was introduced to the contractor we'd be working with and I immediately felt at ease with the woman that had made a name for herself and her company in town. She explained that this was her fourth year working with the alliance and that we were all saints for donating our time.

Quickly we followed her over to the location of house three, where some construction had already begun. This particular house was going to be a reconstruction from the existing frame, not a complete teardown. I had been secretly hoping to destroy something with a sledgehammer, but it seemed as if my vision was nothing more than a pipe dream.

Within the group, I let each person choose which task they wanted to start with, the majority requesting to reframe the structure. Of course, with my luck, that left me on floor duty.

After a quick rundown by the contractor on how to remove the old flooring in each room I went to work. Starting with the bedroom in the back of the house, I began ripping up the carpet, exposing the nails and subfloor. There had been no padding under the old dingy carpet. The movement of the carpet kicked dirt and dust in the air, which left me sneezing even with the mask I was wearing.

I had rolled the mass into the center of the room and stood in the doorway, wondering how I was going to get the pile out by myself.

Wandering outside, I went in search of the contractor or Dr. Fincher, but I didn't see either person. I supposed that I could pull someone from the team to help me haul it to the dumpster, but I didn't want to disturb them from their own projects.

Defeated, I walked back into the house and lifted the edge of the roll of carpet and tugged. The mass didn't want to move at first, but finally, it budged, inch by agonizing inch. I had no idea carpet could weigh so much. I finally got the roll into the hallway, which gave me a direct line out of the front door when I backed into a large mass.

Whirling around, I quickly formed an apology, but the sound died on my lips when I found Archer standing behind me with a pinched expression on his face.

"What are you doing?" he growled, his muscular arms crossed against his chest.

"Ugh, bringing the carpet out to the dumpster."

"By yourself?"

"Ugh. . .yeah?" I replied as if he couldn't see that was exactly what I was doing.

Instead of responding, Archer bent down and grabbed the end of the roll, gesturing with his chin for me to grab the other end.

"You should have asked for help. You're going to get hurt doing this all by yourself."

If he had been anyone else, I would have assumed that he indeed was looking out for my welfare, but with his condescending tone and pinched expression, I knew he was anything but looking out for me.

Biting back at him, I replied, "I would have except everyone was busy with their own assignments and, of course, you were nowhere to be found this morning."

"I was busy." His response was clipped as if he didn't owe me an explanation, which he didn't, but if he was going to have an attitude, I certainly deserved some sort of reasoning.

"Of course you were. Who was the flavor last night?" I questioned as I followed him to the dumpster, immediately regretting that I had accused him of sleeping around last night.

"No one you would know." Together we hefted the pile of old material into the dumpster and I found myself in another sneezing attack. "Now, where is the assignment list so that I can make sure everyone is staying on task?" he demanded and something about his condescending tone sent a wave of fury through me. I had already been disgusted by how he had spoken to Callie yesterday morning, but he had no reason to speak to me in that manner.

"It's in my back pocket for safe keeping," I explained as I walked back into the house, grabbing a hammer along the way to remove the nails left from the carpet. Knowing he was following me, I added, "I can assure you that everyone is staying on task."

"Yes, well, excuse me for not trusting your assurance. My mother put me in charge."

Spinning on my heel, I turned to face him and pointed the end of the hammer in his direction. "I hate to break it to you, but when you didn't show up this morning, your mother put me in charge today. And since your mother is the one in charge, I will be following her directions."

"You're being ridiculous." Archer flung his hands in the air as I went about plucking nails from the subfloor.

"You can take that up with Dr. Fincher. Now, if you'll excuse me, I have work to do." The boy was infuriating as he stomped out of the room like an insolent child that didn't get a toy that he wanted. I didn't have time for the games he played.

Through the window, I watched him stalk across the backyard until he found his mother speaking with the contractors. I couldn't read lips, but I was sure he was telling her how difficult I was and how I wasn't qualified to be in charge for the day. Surprisingly, Dr. Fincher patted Archer's cheek in a lovingly way before she pointed back toward the house, directly to where I was watching through the window.

Sullenly he walked back to the house, his steps less confident than before. I turned away from the window the closer he came and went back to pulling nails from the subfloor. I could tell that he had returned to the bedroom without having to look up from my job. My body could sense his closeness, just as it had at dinner last night.

From under my lashes, I watched as he extricated his own hammer from his tool belt that sat low on his hips and went to the other side of the room and began pulling nails. We worked together in complete silence, the only noise coming from the radio just outside the window.

By the end of the first workday, Archer and I had wordlessly pulled the carpet in the other two remaining bedrooms on the second floor. My body also ached in new places that exercise and dance didn't reach. If this was going to be a daily occurrence during the summer, I would need to buy stock in pain relief.

The following week went the same as the first day, except Archer and I had thrown down a silent gauntlet to see who would be the group leader for the day. I secretly thought that Dr. Fincher and the rest of our team got some sort of sick enjoyment out of our competition. But regardless of who handled the task sheet for the day, Archer and I worked silently to remove the linoleum and rotted hardwood floors throughout the house while the rest of the group worked with the contractor to pull out old drywall and fix any foundation issues. They had found a leak in the basement, which led to digging out around the house and resealing any cracks or fissures in the concrete.

On Friday afternoon, I wanted nothing more than to spread out on the queen-sized bed that had finally arrived almost four days late, but Alice had called to see if I wanted an extra shift due to a stomach virus going around. I readily agreed despite my exhaustion and aches and pains.

Filling my duffle bag with extra clothes and the required lingerie that Alice's company offered a stipend for, I grabbed a frozen burrito from my fridge. I quickly heated it up before leaving my apartment.

As I started to do daily, I glanced back and forth down the hall and then checked the stairwell to see if Archer was anywhere in sight. I could tolerate him on the jobsite since there were other people around the majority of the time, but he never hesitated to throw jabs my way when we were alone. Most of the comments dealing with my lack of style and appearance. Usually, I gave it back just as strong by pointing out his playboy ways and his likelihood of having an STD. We verbally sparred until one of us had enough and stormed off the site. Usually, I got the last word, but occasionally I had to step away to dry the tears that threatened to spill over. But I learned how to deal with his nasty comments, just not at the pace I had hoped. I could barely keep up most days. It's as if he kept a book of insults in his nightstand and memorized a few just for me.

Assuming the coast was clear, I made my way down the stairs then across the hallway. Just when I thought that I had cleared any disastrous meeting, Archer came stomping through the main doors. Our eyes locked and neither of us seemed to be able to pull away. A visual game of chicken took place until I could no longer pin him with my gaze and I turned away. I hated to see that damn smug smile grace his far too gorgeous face. With his bad attitude, he really had no right to be so attractive.

Hiking my duffle bag higher on my shoulder, I braced myself for whatever critique he planned to throw my way. I didn't have to wait long. As I stepped off the last of the stairs, Archer said, "Headed off to go dumpster diving for some more clothes?"

That one stung more than most and I had to bite my cheek to keep from crying in front of him. He didn't know that my family had no money to buy the nice designer clothes that he and his harem favored. I shopped at thrift stores or secondhand stores looking for a bargain. I didn't care what the clothes looked like, just that they were in good condition and would fit.

I moved past him as quickly as I could, but I didn't expect for him to grab my arm to try and stop me.

"Hey. . ." he said with a hint of remorse lacing his words. "I didn't mean-"

"Don't touch me," I bellowed, jerking my arms free from his grasp.

"Sarah, I'm. . ."

"Oh look. You finally learned my name. It only took a week of working next to me. Does that mean I'll no longer be referred to as Freegan?" Which I had learned was sort of a derogatory term for a dumpster diver.

"Don't be a bitch."

"Well, don't be an asshole. I have somewhere to be if you don't mind," I snarled as I tried to move past him again. Luckily, this time I was successful.

I kept replaying the scenario during my walk to the bus station, wondering if his apology had been anywhere close to sincere. From the short time that I've spent with Archer around other people, he was generally in a good mood and was an expert at putting people at ease. People thought he was funny and seemed to enjoy his company. I couldn't figure out why he was so hateful toward me.

Except, as I took my seat on the bus, I remembered the haunted and pained look that grew on his face when I bumped into him at the fundraiser. His face had turned an unhealthy shade of green and he had bolted from the scene before I could even apologize fully.

I'd already had a preconceived notion about Archer from his laughter at my clumsiness, but paired with everything else I had witnessed at his hand, I wasn't sure which Archer was the real one. The one that gave off a broody and angered persona, or the one that seemed to breathe life into everyone else by just being in their presence.

Or maybe the real Archer was hiding beneath the surface. I hadn't decided if I even cared to find out.

RENEE HARLESS

CHAPTER SEVEN

ARCHER

J olting awake, I wiped the sweat away
from my chilled skin. God, it had been
days of the same nightmare over and
over again. No matter what I did to
exhaust myself in the hopes of keeping
the dreams at bay, they were still occurring
over and over again. I couldn't even wake
myself up in the hopes of ending them. The
second I closed my eyes, they would start up
exactly where they left off.

Except these weren't the same dreams
I'd had since I was eight. These dreams
left me screaming in the middle of the
night. I'd relive the scenario where I
found my sister dead in her room,

except when the landlord would arrive, my sister's lifeless body turned into Sarah's. The redheaded woman couldn't even leave me alone in my dreams.

The lack of sleep was leaving me irritable and anxious, all of which I took out on her since she was the one taking part in my nightmares.

Summer rain pounded against the window to my room and, instead of going for a run to clear my mind, I decided to stay in and paint. I had nothing in mind as I pulled out the acrylics, choosing two or three colors to begin the design.

Normally I only painted abstracts or attempted landscapes at best, but this morning I had an unyielding desire to paint a portrait. Perhaps if I painted the face of the woman that I couldn't get out of my mind, I could imprint her on the canvas and rid myself of her. I was hopeful but not confident as I selected my brushes and got to work.

Hours passed and I could hear my brothers bustling around as they woke. They moved around without a single care while I sat here in my closet, struggling to keep myself together.

"Archer?" A soft knock sounded on my bedroom door and it immediately jolted me out of my zone. "I made some sandwiches for lunch," Jolee called out. Man, my brother really lucked out with that one. She made sure to take care of all of us even though we were grown adults.

Setting my paints aside, I thanked her and said that I would be out shortly. Taking a step back out of the closet, I looked over the painting, prepared to critique my own work. Except, as I carefully inspected the canvas, there wasn't anything that I would change. It wasn't perfect, nor did it follow any artistic guidelines, but it was raw and unfiltered and showed every ounce of the emotion I felt when I would wake from the nightmares. Each brushstroke was a piece of my soul. The motions jerky and unclean, but together they made a portrait of pain within the beauty.

I didn't bother washing more than my hands when I stepped into the kitchen, watching as Jolee's eyes widened as she noticed the red droplets all over my arms.

"It's not blood, it's paint," I explained as I grabbed one of the many sandwiches towering on the counter.

"You paint?"

"Sometimes."

"Wow. I had no idea. I'd love to see something sometime," she said as she placed another meat-filled sandwich on the counter.

"I don't show anyone my work," I growled with my mouth stuffed.

"Oh. Well, I bet they're wonderful, and if you change your mind, I'd love to be one of the first."

Quietly I devoured another three sandwiches before rising from the barstool at the counter.

"Thanks for lunch."

With a joyful smile, Jolee replied, "You're welcome," as if I hadn't spoken harshly to her a mere few minutes before.

Trey messaged as I was making my way back to my bedroom, asking if I wanted to join him and some of his other friends for his birthday. They wanted to check out a new club that was a couple of towns over. I had no plans, so I readily agreed, hoping that I'd find another female to bring home.

My night with Callie had left me worrisome, and I hadn't gone out to find a willing partner since then. She had come by the apartment numerous times, and had even begun to stalk me around campus. I worried that soon I would find a dead animal in my bed. She seemed to be off her rocker and unable to comprehend that we were only going to have that one night together.

Ford had even begun to worry that Callie would lash out at Jolee since she lived with us. I promised him that if I saw Callie again, I would make it absolutely certain that things were over. But I couldn't promise that she would listen to reason.

A few hours later, Trey messaged that he was waiting outside. He and his friends had gone all out and rented a limo for his twenty-first birthday. I was grateful to have been invited and planned to buy him a few rounds at the club.

"So, where are we headed?" I asked Trey as I piled in with the four other guys in the back of the limousine.

Despite being able to text coherently, Trey was already feeling the effects of the liquor provided in the vehicle. He stared at me as he tried to come up with the name of the club. Impatiently I turned to one of the other passengers and prompted for the name.

"Bird of Fire or something like that."

Hm. . .I had never heard of it, but I tended to keep close to campus so that there was never any temptation to drive.

"Sounds fun."

"Yeah, the word is the ladies are smokin'."

The way he said the last word had my ears instantly perking up.

"I'm sorry, what kind of club is this again?"

"It's a strip club. I thought Trey told you."

Bile rose in my throat at the thought of stepping foot inside a strip club. I also didn't want to explain why I wanted to go back to my apartment.

"It's supposed to be a real classy place," one of the other guys said. He reminded me of Johnny Bravo with his black shirt and spiked yellow hair. "I've gone with my girlfriend and even she was impressed."

I was going to have to take their word for it.

As the limo pulled into the parking lot, I had lost all ability to breathe or form a coherent thought.

"Hey, man. You okay?" the Johnny Bravo look-alike asked.

"I. . .ugh. . .I'm going to call a rideshare to pick me up. This was a great idea, but I just. . .can't." I left them with no explanation as I dove out of the limo and walked toward the bench where the bus dropped people off and picked them up. I felt bad for leaving Trey on his birthday, but I'd make it up to him later.

I watched the guys struggle to carry a drunk Trey into the club. The bouncer shook his head as he scanned their IDs, pointing to Trey with an angered expression. My guess was that he didn't tolerate rowdy guests and wanted to make sure that his friends kept him in line.

I sat outside on the bench for a few minutes, my stomach growling as I waited for my rideshare. The map showed that they were still a few minutes away, stuck behind an accident.

A bus pulled up to the bench, I stepped back so that the driver didn't think I was there for a ride, but I was still surprised when it stopped. A group of people exited the bus, most turning and crossing the street to go to the market across the way, but one person continued toward the club. The hood of a rain jacket covered her head, but I caught a glimpse of bright red hair.

She made her way toward the back of the building and I began to follow along, only to hear a high-pitched whistle as I passed the entrance.

"Only way in," the bouncer snarled as he crossed his arms against his chest to appear bulkier than he probably was. Except I knew he could kick my ass at the drop of a hat either way.

"Sorry," I apologized as I approached. My hands were sweaty as I got closer and my lungs felt as if I was one breath away from seizing. I was one second away from bolting, but the need to confirm if that was Sarah was too strong.

He scanned my ID after I dropped it on the ground, twice, then let me inside. I had been to the many strip joints when my sister worked the circuit. They weren't the place for a young boy. I remember the walls lined with paneling or dilapidated décor. And they always smelled of smoke, booze, and sex.

But this place was nothing like what I remembered. The walls were lined in decadent fabrics and the tables were spotless. Even the bar area looked well-kept. Color me impressed as I looked around the room.

A woman in a business suit stood off in the corner with a phone in her hand. Her hair pulled back in a severe bun. She would be attractive under any other circumstances, but my mind was locked in on the woman I saw get off the bus.

From the corner of my eye, I saw Trey and his friends piled in a booth close to the stage. They were laughing, but they seemed to be behaving themselves. I wondered if they were the reason the woman in the suit was close by. The rest of the clientele were men in business suits and women dressed as if they just left the runway.

I couldn't comprehend the differences between this club and the ones my sister worked at. They had to all be the same, deep within the bones. Money, drugs, and sex were what fueled the industry, that I was certain.

From the edge of the stage, I noticed a fabric-covered door that I was certain led to the club's backstage area. I inched my way toward it, following the perimeter of the room, until I watched the severe woman turn to speak with the bartender. Then I made my move. I opened the door just wide enough to slip through then I had to give my eyes a few minutes to adjust to the dim lighting.

When I took a step farther into the space, I noticed a series of doors lined against the wall. It took only a second to realize that these were private rooms. My sister had spoken about them and the higher amount of money a stripper could earn.

The bile I had tamped down from earlier rose to a higher level. I was seriously afraid that I was going to find myself covering the floor in vomit if I didn't find Sarah soon.

"What are you doing back here?" the stoic woman from earlier commanded as she stepped through the door.

"I'm looking for Sarah."

"Boyfriend or customer?" she asked as if either was a common occurrence. My jaw ticked at the thought of anyone being either option.

"Neither. Concerned friend."

"Sure don't look like any friend I know. She's scheduled next, so you can see yourself back out to the main area unless you want to pay for a private room."

I was tempted, far more than I should have been, to pay for a private room, just to convince her that she was making a mistake.

"I'll wait. Thanks," I grumbled as I turned around.

"Don't go causing trouble, understand?" she said in a tone that meant that she wasn't messing around.

"Understood."

I made my way back to the main room and kept walking until I reached the bar. I had no desire to watch Sarah strut on stage, but I had every intention of waiting until the club closed to speak to her.

I ordered a vodka tonic and kept my back to the stage as the music started. A rock song pulsed through the speakers and I closed my eyes, trying to stop from turning around. I could imagine her moving her hips and legs to the beat of the song. Her hair would swing with every motion and she would caress her own skin with her hands, leaving the watchers wishing that they were the ones touching her.

I wasn't sure how long I sat at the club. At one point, the manager or owner nodded in my direction, most likely pleased that I behaved myself. I had even stayed longer than Trey and his friends. I didn't want to think about them drooling over Sarah.

Overhead lights began to flicker and I took that as the cue that the club was closing.

"She's headed toward the bus," the blonde woman said as she stepped behind the bar.

"Thank you. . ." I said, prompting her for her name.

"Alice."

Nodding I left a hefty tip on the bar and exited through the front with the other customers. I didn't see Sarah at first, but from around the corner she approached with her hood pulled over her head.

"Sarah!" I called out and her head jerked up in surprise. Her eyes widened as I approached and as I took a hold of her arm and pulled her away from the crowd over to the a shadowed area of the parking lot I noticed that her breaths were coming faster.

"What are you doing here?" she seethed as she jerked her arm away.

"Me? What am I doing here? What the hell are you doing here? Do you know what kind of place this is? What goes on at places like this?"

"I do. The question is, do you?" she retorted as she crossed her arms in defiance.

"I know better than anyone. You know I would never have suspected this from you. God does Jolee know that her friend is a druggie and a whore?" The words fumbled form my mouth before I could pull them back in. Sarah jumped back as if I had slapped her.

"How dare you. I have nothing to say to you. Please don't follow me home."

Without a comeback, Sarah rushed toward the bus stop, and as if by a miracle, the bus pulled up only a moment later.

I was left standing in the dark, wondering why I had called her those things, but they were all I knew of the business. It was what had darkened the light of my sister and eventually killed her. My only remaining question was why Sarah needed to work here at all.

RENEE HARLESS

CHAPTER EIGHT

SARAH

I stewed the entire bus ride home. I had never in my life been accused of such awful things. I knew that some people wouldn't understand my dancing or the reason why I needed to work at the club, but of all people, I hadn't expected it from Archer. He himself was a manwhore of epic proportions.

What made what he did any different from what I did, except I got paid to use my body. And I didn't have to worry about any aftermath.

I was almost expecting to find Archer or Jolee waiting outside of my apartment when I arrived home but was pleasantly surprised that I got to avoid that confrontation. Inside I dropped my duffle bag onto the floor and immediately rushed toward the shower. I didn't feel dirty from the club, but from the awful words Archer had called me.

He was so adamant about the accusations and I stood under the spray of the hot water, wondering if this had to do with something from his past. It made the most sense, but I didn't have a reason to ask around or to pry. I could just hope that he kept his distance and didn't show up again at Phoenix's Fire.

I tossed and turned throughout the night, and by the time morning had arrived, I was worse for the wear. Wellington Housing Alliance expected me to arrive today, but I was within an inch of not showing up. But I couldn't give Archer that satisfaction.

Just to be on the safe side, I grabbed a pair of noise-canceling headphones hoping that he would take the hint and stay away from me for the day.

Except my luck must have been running out because when I arrived, Dr. Fincher was teaming us up to work on special projects. Fate being the bitch that she is, Archer and I were paired together to install the cabinets in the kitchen. It made me wonder if this was some sort of sick joke to him. He probably convinced his mom to pair us together on purpose.

Except laid out on a buffet table in the house, Archer set up a slew of donuts, scones, and coffee for the workers. It was a sweet gesture that didn't match the condescending man from the night before.

Grabbing one of the cabinets, I lifted it up as best as I could, which meant it was only an inch off the ground, but I carried its weight across the grass and into the house where Archer waited with a sketch of the kitchen layout.

"I brought some music today. Maybe you can dance for all of us," he said as he stood with his hands perched on his hips. Even with his hate-filled words, I couldn't help but admire the way he looked from behind.

Stupid hormones.

Without a word, I spun on my heels and went to retrieve another cabinet, leaving Archer to compile a list of grievances against me.

"You know, it would be nice if you could help," I told him as I placed another cabinet in the kitchen. I had brought inside all but two of the cabinets and my arms and back were protesting.

"But you seem to have it all under control. I didn't think you needed my help. Maybe we could call one of those bouncers from the club to lift all of the heavy things for you."

Rolling my eyes, I went back outside and finished bringing in the cabinets as Archer moved them around the kitchen to match the sketch from the contractor.

"Do you think there is enough space in here?" Archer asked, and I hesitated at first, waiting for the insult, but as he remained silent, I took a second to look around the kitchen. It was spacious for the small bungalow. "I mean, why don't you go ahead and perform for us and we can get some perspective?"

Whirling around on him, I stared at Archer with a hatred I had never experienced. Sure I danced to make money but that gave him no right to ridicule and attack me because he thought I was selling my body.

"What the fuck is your problem, Archer? Why do you care so much that I dance to make money? I have to and the only people that matter understand. So, tell me, why do you care so much? Why do you care if I stand on a stage and take my clothes off? Why do you care if I make more in one night than I have in my entire life? Why do you ca-"

Suddenly his lips were on mine in a kiss that spoke of hunger, yearning, and desire. His hand snaked around my neck and up into my hair, his hold controlling my movements. He titled my head to the side and he pushed his tongue past my lips and I eagerly twisted my tongue around his.

"Fuck," he growled against my mouth as he reached down to tug my shirt free from my denim shorts.

I was lost in the moment, lost in the feeling and possession by Archer. His hand skimmed across the skin of my stomach as he gripped my waist and I sucked in a breath at the contact.

Footsteps sounded down the hallway and Archer quickly pulled his mouth away from mine and I immediately missed the contact. Our chests heaved in unison with stares that questioned what was happening. But before we could come to a conclusion, Archer moved backward, pulling me along with him until we were in the small bathroom right next to the kitchen.

Locking the door, Archer spun me around until my back pressed against the cold wood. He retook ownership of my lips, using his tongue to gain entrance into my mouth. My hands immediately went to the hem of his work shirt and I pushed it upward, gliding my fingers against his washboard abs along the way.

With every second that passed, his breath became more erratic until he sounded like a feral beast ready to break free from his confines.

Arched pulled his mouth away again for a second time and I immediately protested until he stood back and yanked his shirt over his head, revealing a chest that could rival Captain America's.

"Damn," I murmured as I drank him in. Quickly he grabbed my shirt and yanked it over my head, my hair falling around me in a mess of waves and I forgot how to speak as he leaned forward and pressed an open-mouth kiss against the swell of my breast pushed upward from the simple cotton bra that I wore.

With fumbling fingers, I undid the waistband of his cargo shorts, slipping them down his thighs with his boxers. My body was in a rage and the only solution was to own Archer's body the way he was taking over mine.

I wrapped my hand around Archer's impressive length at the same time he gripped my chin in his hand, holding my head still.

"We shouldn't be doing this," he said as he pressed an angry kiss against my lips and then pulled back. "I fucking hate knowing that anyone can go into that club and watch you show off your body."

"It's not up to you," I argued as I squeezed his cock slightly, growing addicted to the moan I received from him in response.

"Like hell, it isn't. You're mine for right now, Sarah. Do you understand?"

"I'm not playing your games, Archer," I explained as he released my chin and dove for the button of my shorts. My head collided with the door as he slipped his hand beneath my panties and found my damp center. "I won't be one of many in your gaslighting schemes. That's a game I won't play."

"No games. Just right now, then we can go back to hating each other," he clarified as he slid a digit into my slit. My body arched toward him in response, my breasts pressing against his bare chest.

"Everything is a game to you. Now stop talking and fuck me already."

I wasn't sure when I had grown so bold, but Archer followed my command and pushed down my shorts, exposing me to him.

From his wallet, he pulled out a condom and guided it down his shaft before wrapping his arm around my waist and hoisting me higher against the door.

"Keep quiet," he groaned as he slid my body down onto his shaft. We moaned in unison, and somewhere in the back of my mind, I feared that someone would overhear our tryst, but my body was in too heady of a state to care.

"Fuck, feels too good."

One of his hands left my thigh and slammed against the door as his thrusts grew wild and rough.

"Oh. Oh," I moaned as I felt my orgasm closing in. Archer reached between us, relying on my legs wrapped around his waist to stay up, and rubbed small circles around my clit until I exploded in his arms. Archer quickly followed with his own release, then surprised me as he pressed a kiss against my shoulder before setting me back onto my feet.

Words weren't exchanged as we dressed in silence. I wasn't sure what to say to him, and from the way he was yanking on his clothes, I was sure that Archer was left speechless as well.

It was now awkward. I shouldn't have been surprised. The man that called me a whore had just used me as one and that realization left my lower lids watering.

"Sarah, I. . ." Archer began, but I was growing too distraught to listen.

"Can you finish the kitchen layout? I need to get home."

"Yeah, but maybe we should talk."

"I have nothing to say. You proved your point. Thanks for making me feel exactly like you insulted."

"Sarah."

Twisting the knob on the door, I exited with a flourish, not making contact with anyone as I left the construction site and made my way back to my apartment. I should have ridden the bus, but the walk helped me to clear my head.

Archer was wrong about me. He accused me of things I hadn't ever done until today. I had never let someone use my body the way that he had. Even though I had consented to every kiss and every touch. I wanted him as badly as he had wanted me. But afterward, I felt dirty and used, especially knowing that it would only be the one time.

I finally made it back to my complex a bit worse for wear and it took an incredible amount of strength to make it up the stairs. The walk back hadn't helped me clear my mind as I had hoped. Instead, I was left considering moving back home. I had a hard enough time fitting in with the other students at Wellington. If rumors started swirling about me dancing or being one of Archer's many quests, I wasn't sure that I could handle it.

A familiar blonde came into view when I approached the landing for my floor and I recognized Callie standing outside my door.

"Can I help you?" I asked and she swirled around with hatred in her eyes.

"You're the reason he won't give me the time of day."

"I'm sorry, who are you talking about?"

"Archer. We. . .we had an incredible night together and then you showed up and everything fell apart."

I looked at her in confusion. I wasn't sure what planet she fell from, but she was absolutely delusional if she thought for a second that I had anything to do with Archer's games.

"I think you're confused. Archer played a game and you fell for it hook, line, and sinker. He makes you believe that you're the reason he didn't want anything more. It's all a mind game."

"You're lying," she fumed as she took a step closer to me.

"I'm not, but believe what you want."

I stepped around her and prayed that she didn't retaliate behind my back.

"He won't be with you, you know!" she shouted. "He doesn't date whores."

Well, it was the second time I had been called that today. At least the universe was consistent.

"You're right. He doesn't. Take that as a hint," I said as I slammed my apartment door in her face.

I took a deep breath and let the calmness of my apartment wash over me. This was my haven, my safe space, and no one could question or ridicule my decisions. I was exhausted after my trek home and tossed my body onto the top of my bed, turning my head to gaze around the small living space I had created.

The credenza stood out in its green façade with brass pulls. I had completely transformed the piece from something dull and lifeless to a really beautiful piece of art. I was proud of my work on the furniture and the work I had done on myself.

Archer's words had hit home for me, but only because I knew that there was something in his past that was causing him to lash out at me. There was a dread that played onto everyone of Archer's fears. I couldn't imagine living my life in that way.

CHAPTER NINE

ARCHER

S hock.

There was no other way to describe how I felt as I finished installing the cabinets in the house Sarah and I had been working on. I felt like a filthy, dirty human being that took advantage of a situation.

I had been angry, so furious that everything I saw in my vision was in vivid colors of red. It reminded me of the paintings in my closet.

With her pure, innocent heart, Sarah had let me possess her in a way that I had never done with anyone before. I was filled with so much fury at the thought of anyone watching her dance on a stage, watching her body sway to the music while wearing nothing more than silk and lace, that I had an uncontrollable need to own her.

And she had let me. She had matched me kiss for kiss. I had thought her the pawn in my game of control, the weakest out of us. But she was proving to be the bishop, the one to watch, the one that could make any move and capture the other player.

She had captured me alright.

The rest of the afternoon she was all that I could think about. And the more I thought about why I had this overwhelming desire to be with Sarah, the more I realized that she had captivated me from the start.

She had seemed weak at first when I watched her trip and fall on campus, but looking back, she had been so strong. She had ignored the snickers and held her head high as she kept moving along.

And she didn't take any crap from me either, despite how cruel my words had been.

I was completely taken by her. An affection that had grown by each day as we worked side by side on the house project.

Normally I had a plan in place when it came to women, but this time when it really mattered, I was at a loss. How could I convince her that I wanted more than just the one moment together? How could I convince her that she was worth more than the few thousand she made dancing on a stage?

Could I even compete with the money?

"Hi, Archer. You're here late this evening."

My mother stepped foot into the kitchen and glanced around the project that was coming together nicely.

"Yeah, I wanted to finish this up."

"You've done a great job. Where's Sarah?"

"She. . .ugh. . .asked if she could leave," I said as I went back to screwing in one of the cabinet doors.

"What did you do, Archer Samuel?"

"Me? How do you know that I did anything?" Damn her for having a sixth sense about relationships.

She knew about Jolee and Ford before they had even come out.

"Because I saw the way you looked at her when you thought no one was looking."

"Yeah? And what way is that?"

"Like you love her."

"Love her? Mom, I've known her only a couple of weeks." Let's not mention that I royally pissed her off, accused her of something she had never done, and then took advantage of a situation.

"I fell in love with Adam in only a couple of hours. Would it help you to know that she looks at you the same way?"

"Maybe. It's just. . .I screwed up. Big time. And I don't think that there is a way to fix it."

"I'm not surprised. Sometimes you boys act before you think. You have been that way since you joined the family. Archer, the thing about you is that you have one of the biggest hearts that I know. You just need to open yourself up to her. It's that simple."

"And what if that isn't enough?"

"Then you keep trying. You'll find a way."

"Thanks, Mom," I said, wrapping her in a tight hug.

"And don't forget, you have someone at your disposal that would be more than willing to make sure you and her friend end up together."

"Jolee," I murmured. If anyone could help me convince Sarah to give me a chance, it was her closest friend.

"See? I told you that you were bright. Now, why don't you get out of here?"

"Yes, ma'am," I said just as the contractor came in to inspect the work done for the day.

Once I got back to the apartment, I had a plan of sorts in place, but I needed Jolee more than ever. Ford was sitting on the couch when I arrived and I asked where his second half was. He pointed toward his bedroom and I made my way in that direction, knocking on the door.

"Hey. Sorry, I'm just folding clothes. What's up?" I followed her into Ford's room. Jealousy arose in me at their domesticated bliss and I wondered if I would ever have that, if I even deserved it.

"I need help. . .with Sarah."

"What about Sarah?" she asked as she set down the shirt she had been folding and sat down on the edge of the bed.

"Did you know that she-"

"Dances at Phoenix's Fire? Yes, I promised her I'd come to watch one night when she was ready. How did you find out?"

"I was there by accident and when I saw her go inside the building I. . .I may have overreacted."

I went on to explain our fight that night and what happened at the jobsite today, leaving out specific details. I felt even worse after reliving it a second time.

"Oh, Archer. You're better than that. You didn't even give her a chance to explain, not that she should have to."

"I know that you're right. I just felt out of control when I saw her there. It didn't make sense to me and it brought back memories from my childhood that I try to keep at bay."

"Look, I won't say that I begin to understand what you or your brothers have been through. Each of you has some sort of horror that haunts you every waking second. But you can't use that as an excuse to treat a good and kind person so poorly. She had a choice to make and it took a lot of courage for her to choose the path that she did.

"Sarah can tell you herself, but it's not a secret. She was a recipient of the Hastings Scholarship, the one that has been revoked since Ford's father passed away. The school wants full tuition by the beginning of the next semester."

Because I was the adoptive son of a Wellington University professor, my brothers and I went to the college for a very small amount. Most of us had some sort of academic scholarship that covered tuition and our off-campus housing. We were one of the lucky few, but I knew the cost of tuition for the private college and I knew that a normal student wouldn't have access to funds of that amount.

And like a case of whiplash, I understood the lengths Sarah had gone to keep up with her education.

"I'm an idiot."

"I wouldn't say that, but you need to know that she isn't ashamed of the job. I think she's actually a little proud of it. When I first met her, I thought she was this shy, timid, little hermit. She's definitely come out of her shell."

"What should I do? I'm not sure she's going to be willing to hear my apology."

"Just be honest. That's all you can do. But, for the love of all that is holy, do not. And I repeat, do not, give her an ultimatum. It will not end well for you."

"You give good advice, Jolee."

"I know. Now, if only I could get your brother to listen to me every once in a while," she added with a giggle.

Before heading to Sarah's apartment to grovel, I had a plan to put into place. I went into my room and set things in motion. I was going to bear everything to her and hoped that she'd forgive me or at least consider it.

CHAPTER TEN

SARAH

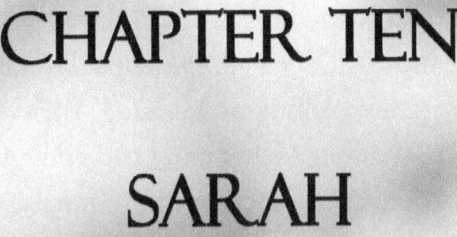

It had been three days since I had seen Archer. I pretended like I didn't care, but deep down, I missed him.

I missed the snarky comebacks.

I missed the teasing.

I missed the way he thought he was superior but always gave way and let me lead.

I just missed him.

I kept reliving that one incredible and explosive moment of reckless abandon with him in my mind. Nothing had ever been as wild, chaotic, and perfect as that moment in the bathroom.

I could never look at the house the same way again.

Rain had poured for the days since I left him, keeping me tucked into the apartment and unable to volunteer with the Wellington Housing Alliance. It was my only connection to Archer and I had enough pride that I wasn't about the knock on the door to his apartment.

Yet.

I was wearing down and had thought of countless excuses to see him. But I feared that he didn't want to see me.

Maybe Callie had been right and I was just another girl on his list. Another pawn in his game. He had me in checkmate and I saw no way out.

To keep my mind occupied, I worked on refinishing the small table and chairs I found near the dumpster outside our complex. I waited to see if anyone would claim the furniture, but I snagged it and carried it up to my place when it sat for a few hours.

The table and chairs were old and worn. Nothing that I couldn't breathe new life into with a bit of TLC and stain.

Pulling my hair into a sloppy mass on the top of my head, I twisted the hem of my shirt into a knot to keep it from getting in the way and began sanding the piece.

The noise from the sander was loud enough to drown out the music I had playing on the stereo. It wasn't until I took a break for some water that I realized that someone was knocking on my door. I hoped that it wasn't the neighbors again. I kept to my promise of only using power tools during waking hours instead of late at night, which was unfortunate because that was my favorite time to work on the pieces.

"Coming!" I shouted as I turned down the volume on the radio and brushed the sanding dust from my shirt and shorts.

I opened the door to my apartment with a flourish and froze when I saw Archer standing on the other side carrying two large canvases under his arms.

"Archer? What are you doing here?"

"Can I come in, please? I want to talk to you about some things."

"Yeah, I mean. Sure, you can come in."

He stepped in behind me and waited for me to shut the door. I could smell the cologne he wore. Something rich and musky that tickled my nose just a bit. It was a scent that was all Archer Calloway.

"Sorry for the mess," I said as I gestured for him to come farther inside and take a seat on the couch. "Can I get you a water, beer, anything?"

"No, thank you. Just sit beside me, please."

He sounded as defeated as I felt.

"So, what brings you here?" I asked after a minute had passed where Archer seemed to be studying my apartment.

"At first, I came to apologize, but then I realized that it would do little to no good. Then I figured that there was something more that I needed to do than just to apologize. I needed to share a part of me with you."

"I. . .I don't understand."

"I like you, Sarah, a lot. You changed the rules of the game for me. No longer do I want just one night to forget my past. I want every night, with you, to remind me how far I've come."

"I'm lost, Archer."

"Here, I just want you to listen."

And listen, I did. He spent about an hour describing in horrific detail how his parents had died and his sister took care of him until she could no longer take care of herself. She had stripped to make money, then the pull from drugs and prostitution became too much and had been the end of everything for them. He had gone days without anyone as his sister lay dead in her bedroom. If it wasn't for a persistent landlord, there was no telling how long he would have been locked in the apartment.

Archer went into details about the nightmares that plagued him and how they had recently morphed into images of me lying lifeless in the apartment.

By the time he was done telling his story, we were both in tears. He mourned the life of his family and I mourned the innocence that Archer had lost.

Everything made sense then—the fear of me dancing, the hostility at my defiance. Everything clicked into place.

Then he showed me a piece of himself that no one had ever seen. The canvases were beautiful. One angry and one peaceful. True yin and yangs that were a way of Archer releasing his emotions. He asked me to keep them, to treasure these small parts of his soul that he painted onto the canvases and any part of me that had been hesitant with my feelings fell completely over the cliff in love with him.

"There is one more thing, and then I'll leave you alone."

I didn't want him to leave, but I knew that he might need some time alone after sharing so much of himself.

"Okay."

"I know about the scholarship that you lost. I can't believe that they gave you such a ridiculous timeline for payment. I would have come by a few days ago, but I was busy doing research and trying to gain more information."

Reaching into his back pocket, Archer produced a folded manila envelope and handed it to me.

"Inside you'll find about ten scholarships that you're eligible for as an out-of-state student. Some are small; others are significant enough that, combined, would be more than what you owe."

"You. . .you did this for me?"

"With the help of Jolee, of course. She was the one that called some of the local businesses and inquired about the scholarship funds."

"I can't believe it."

Quickly he added, "This doesn't mean I'm trying to keep you from dancing. I just wanted you to know that it's not the only option. You can do both if you want."

"You'd be okay with that?" I asked. "Now that I know why you're so against the dancing, I don't want you to worry."

"Sarah, as long as I could have you, I'd be okay with anything."

Everything that I had feared was instantly washed away, leaving me feeling refreshed and renewed, just like the credenza that I had breathed new life into.

Not only was I going to be able to stay at the university, I was going to get the guy that made my heart skip beats and my stomach flip over itself. The guy who hid behind a bad attitude but gave me glimpses of the sweet man he could be.

"I can't believe this is happening. I never expected that I'd fall for you or that you'd even look twice at me," I told him as I curled my body against his on the couch.

"Believe it, Sarah. Until I met you, I had no idea how I was living my life. You showed me that every move had a purpose, every thought had an action. You, Sarah Hodges, are my endgame.

EPILOGUE

ARCHER

"**T**his is the last of the boxes," I called out as I sat the box of paint in the corner of the studio apartment.

Once Sarah and I had decided to give our relationship a go, I couldn't be without her for a single night. She changed everything for me. Not only how I treated her and how I lived my life, but my nightmares had ended. The only dreams I had now were those of Sarah walking toward me in a white dress with her long red hair blowing the breeze.

"Oh. Perfect. All of your paint

supplies will fit perfectly in the hutch I picked up."

My girl was so talented when it came to refinishing junky furniture that I had been after her to consider opening up a shop online selling her finds. She was still dead set on working in accounting, but I was adamant that she was missing her calling.

"I grabbed the mail on the way in," I told her. There had been a large white envelope that I hoped was a response to one of her scholarship requests.

With the same amount of excitement a child had on Christmas, Sarah rushed over to the kitchen counter and tore open the envelope. Quietly she read the letter, her face giving nothing away.

"So, what does it say?"

"I got it," she whispered at first. "I got the scholarship from the Wellington Ridge Township."

"Which one is that?" I asked, but I remembered. This was the one that would cover her tuition, books, and living expenses. Roughly seventy thousand dollars an academic year. The best part was that the scholarship would stay with her for the remainder of the time that she was attending Wellington Ridge University.

"The big one. Archer, I can't believe this! If it wasn't for you researching all of these, I'd forever feel like I was just scraping by. Now I can relax and take a breath."

"That's all I want for you. To understand your worth and to feel as if you can do anything."

"What can I ever do to thank you?" she asked coyly as she placed the paper back on the counter and reached out for me, the tips of her fingers hooking into the belt loop of my shorts.

"I'm sure we can come up with something," I said as I leaned toward her and sealed our mouths together as I walked backward toward the bed. She may be the one that got the scholarship, but I was definitely the one who felt like I had won the lottery.

***

Swirling my glass of vodka tonic, I relaxed back in my seat and watched the customers stroll into the room.

The music began to change and I recognized the song, my cock instantly growing hard, knowing my girl was about to go on stage. One of the many perks to being a dancer's boyfriend was that she frequently tried out her new routines on me. I was always happy to oblige her requests.

From the corner of my eye, I saw Alice walk into the main area. We acknowledged each other with a nod and I went back to watching Sarah take the stage.

She amazed me as she swayed to the music, so far removed from the clumsy girl that ran into our coffee table on a daily basis.

"Wow," Jolee whispered from beside me, finally taking Sarah up on the offer to visit the club.

"She's really talented, but I may be biased."

"No, she really is. I didn't even know hips could move that way."

"Oh, they can. And she can bend her legs-" I started, but Jolee slapped her hand across my mouth to stop from telling her more. With all the times I heard her and Ford going at it at night, she deserved a little payback.

We stayed for the rest of the set until Sarah walked out into the club wearing her typical oversized shirt and shorts.

Jolee praised her which caused Sarah to blush, my favorite color on her skin. I still had trouble convincing myself that she was mine and that I would get to spend every day with this beautiful soul.

"Ready to go home, gorgeous?"

"With you, I'd go anywhere."

RENEE HARLESS

STAY IN TOUCH

Newsletter: http://bit.ly/2WokAjS

Author Page: www.facebook.com/authorreneeharless

Reader Group: http://bit.ly/31AGa3B

Instagram: www.instagram.com/renee_harless

Bookbub: www.bookbub.com/authors/renee-harless

Goodreads: http://bit.ly/2TDagOn

Amazon: http://bit.ly/2WsHhPq

Website: www.reneeharless.com

ACKNOWLEDGMENTS

Thank you to all of the readers and bloggers that shared their excitement for this book and series. I hope that Archer and Sarah gave you the love story that you were hoping for.

Patricia thank you so much for the late nights and long days. Without you this book wouldn't have been possible.

To my family, your support has meant more than you'll ever know. Writing while renovating and having a new baby was definitely not something that I expected, but seeing your beautiful faces every day made it all worth it. I love you all so much, every day.

ABOUT THE AUTHOR

Renee Harless is a romance writer with an affinity for wine and a passion for telling a good story.

Renee Harless, her husband, and children live in Blue Ridge Mountains of Virginia. She studied Communication, specifically Public Relations, at Radford University.

Growing up, Renee always found a way to pursue her creativity. It began by watching endless runs of White Christmas- yes even in the summer – and learning every word and dance from the movie. She could still sing "Sister Sister" if requested. In high school, she joined the show choir and a community theatre group, The Troubadours. After marrying the man of her dreams and moving from her hometown she sought out a different artistic outlet – writing.

To say that Renee is a romance addict would be an understatement. When she isn't chasing her kids around the house, working her day job, or writing, she jumps head first into a romance novel.